To Bill

TRACKING

AN OBSESSION FOR TRUTH

my neighbor and friend

BARBARA NELSON

Barbara

Bloomington, IN    authorHOUSE®   Milton Keynes, UK

5-21-07

AuthorHouse™
1663 Liberty Drive, Suite 200
Bloomington, IN 47403
www.authorhouse.com
Phone: 1-800-839-8640

AuthorHouse™ UK Ltd.
500 Avebury Boulevard
Central Milton Keynes, MK9 2BE
www.authorhouse.co.uk
Phone: 08001974150

First published by AuthorHouse 5/7/2007

ISBN: 978-1-4343-0839-9 (sc)

Library of Congress Control Number: 2007903400

Printed in the United States of America
Bloomington, Indiana

This book is printed on acid-free paper.

To my friend, Klara with a K, and Sara and David.

Also to the memories of the annihilation of millions of victims during the Holocaust.

CHAPTER ONE

A strong gust of dark gray smoke ascending from a small corner lot in the curve caught Jennifer's attention as she picked up her pace jogging along Hill Lane. She was taking a short cut, rounding the corner to the parkway that leads to her street. She had taken a longer route and lost track of time. The night is warm, a little muggy, and approaching darkness. The street lights are dim.

Inspired by the romance of the luxury homes and compelling beauty of the vibrant burst of azaleas, dogwoods and redbuds, Jennifer jogged along Hill Lane rather than taking her regular path through the apple-blossom-lined trails of Cobb Park. The park that some say was named after Ty Cobb, a baseball great and former Georgia resident, is popular among local joggers. Its natural scenery was preserved for public recreation, with walks and benches. It is late summer in 2004.

Compelled to investigate the origin of the smoke and notify the proper authorities if necessary, she dashed across the parkway and was horrified to see a man, bloody from head to toe and trapped under a motorcycle. His helmet was covering his face. Immediately, she stomped around in the brush to extinguish the threat of fire. She then hovered over the seemingly lifeless body and cautiously lifted the front of his helmet. With an impaired enervative force, he was able to whisper,

1

"Please get help." Thankfully, he is alive. Jennifer, a surgical nurse at the local Memorial Hospital, checked for vital signs and for hemorrhaging after calling 911.

"My name is David Barr," he told her. Recognizing the name, she is aware this is not a gang member from Macon nor is he any longer a resident of their small community of Middleton, Georgia.

To her recollection, David Barr moved away eight years prior after his father, Dr. Avery Barr, world-renowned plastic surgeon, found by his man-servant in his garage, had been brutally murdered by an unknown assailant. David, home from college on spring break, although considered at the time to be a suspect, was devastated at the news.

Jennifer gently stroked the forehead of David Barr, assuring him he would be all right while they waited for what seemed to be an eternity. She remembered him as a young blonde boy she had seen when visiting Dr. Barr's office with her mother.

Jennifer found a broken branch and carefully placed a splint on his right leg, which was obviously fractured. The right trouser leg was torn, revealing a deep gash that had coagulated. He appeared to be choking on blood from internal injuries. "I am just going to clear your mouth and move your head slightly," she whispered. "Please, you must not try to move." David did not respond. His breathing was shallow. "Where is that ambulance?" Jennifer is impatient now. Just then, a siren was blasting in the distance. She ran to the edge of the grass, waving her small blue flashlight that she always carried on her keychain, shouting to the paramedics, "Help! Over here."

Eric Hawkins and Julie Miller hurriedly scurried, carrying a gurney to the injured man. Recognizing Jennifer Aldrich as a nurse from Memorial, they asked, "What have we here?"

"I didn't see the accident, but he has a broken right leg, a severe gash on the left leg, and internal bleeding. No indication of head injuries. The helmet is intact and he was vocal when I arrived." Eric and Julie used their equipment to take his vitals, looked up at Jennifer in a negative response, and quickly proceeded to get David to the hospital emergency room.

Jennifer knew that Eric and Julie were not employees of EMS and may not have remembered when the story broke about Dr. Barr's vicious murder. She rode in the compartment with the injured David, constantly assuring him he is safe.

CHAPTER TWO

On the way to the hospital, Jennifer couldn't help thinking what would have happened to David. How long would he have gone undiscovered if she hadn't lost track of time taking in the ambience of the scenery? When it started to get dark, she had opted to take a short cut, anxious to reach the comfort of her modest two-bedroom condominium on Winter Street. The small elite suburb of Middleton, northeast of Macon, Georgia, is located on the Ocmulgee River and relatively crime-free, but she is always aware not to put herself in jeopardy. Occasionally, a threat of intrusion by some of the nearby Macon lawbreakers can be a disturbance. Macon is forty miles away and is an industrial city of a much larger population of over 107,000, which produces building and farm materials in addition to textiles, fruits, and pecans. Several of Middleton's residents commute to Macon, having found better opportunities of employment.

Once they arrived in the emergency room, Jennifer located Dr. Jon Vogel, a respected surgeon who she knew was a friend of the Barr family. Dr. Vogel, ready to leave the hospital, decided to stay when the urgent call came in. He asked Jennifer to call David's mother as soon as possible.

"Hello, Mrs. Eva Barr?"

"Yes, I am Mrs. Barr."

"My name is Jennifer Aldrich. I am a nurse at Memorial Hospital. Your son, David, has been in an accident. He is in the emergency room at Memorial Hospital and needs immediate medical attention. David will need you to speak for him. I will give you details when you reach the hospital. Do you have a way to get to the hospital?"

Mrs. Barr, panic in her voice, said, "Yes! I will leave right away."

When David's mother arrived, Jennifer was waiting to escort her to the emergency room. An elegantly dressed petite woman with slightly graying hair, looking to be in her sixties and frantically anxious, arrived by a chauffeur-driven Cadillac. "Are you Mrs. Barr?"

"Yes, please take me to David." Upon seeing her son in such a co-matose state, Eva Barr had to steady herself.

"Eva." Dr. Jon Vogel, a tall, confident, masculine, but gentle man appeared in green scrubs, and took her hand in both of his. "You know that I will do everything possible for David. We know from the x-rays that he has a fractured leg, but the urgency centers on possible internal injuries. I will know more after additional tests are completed."

Eva Barr choked back tears. "Jon, please save my son."

It is now 9:00 p.m.; Jennifer is concerned about Fox, her Australian Shepherd that usually accompanies her when jogging. However, she is reluctant to leave a seemingly frail woman, with whom she has no ties, except having tried to save her son.

"Mrs. Barr, do you have family that you can call to be with you?"

"No, I am a widow. David is my only child and my only relative here. My sister lives in New York." Just then, Dr. Vogel comes out to up-date Mrs. Barr about her son. He puts his arm around her shoulder.

"Eva, I am taking David to surgery. He has a ruptured spleen and a puncture in his transverse colon. We will need to operate immediately. We have been giving him transfusions. You know that I am good at what I do and I will be doing the best work that I can." Having heard this, Jennifer knew she could not leave this devastated woman.

"Mrs. Barr, I want you to know that when I first came upon David after the accident, he was able to give me his name. His helmet had not been damaged. I feel that with God's help through Dr. Vogel, David can recover. Would you like to go to the chapel?"

"Yes! Yes, I would."

Chapter Three

It was almost 2:00 a.m. before Jon Vogel, still in his scrubs, came into the waiting lounge. "Eva, David is stable and in recovery. It is too early to predict a prognosis, but the surgery went well. He will be closely monitored throughout the next twenty-four hours. I know you will not want to leave the hospital," he told her. "I have made arrangements for you to rest in a private room on the next floor. I know Nurse Aldrich will see that you have anything you need before she leaves." After having heard this, Jennifer escorted Mrs. Barr to a comfortable bedroom with a sitting area. The room is reserved for relatives of VIP patients and is equipped with toiletries needed. Jennifer provided a hospital gown and her phone number before she said her goodbyes and assured Eva Barr that her only child is in the best of care. The tension in Eva's expression did not leave.

It is approaching 3:00 a.m. on Sunday morning when Jennifer, after getting a ride from Julie the paramedic, opened the door to her small, tastefully decorated home on Winter Street. Fox, obviously missing the jog with his mistress and eager to go outside, galloped through the open door. Fox has few accidents inside.

Thankfully, this is not the weekend for Nurse Aldrich to be on duty.

Surgeries scheduled during the week make for a more productive pace. However, emergency surgeries happen occasionally. She took a quick shower, dried her hair, and put on some sweats. It is going to feel good to snuggle up with a good book to unwind and eventually fall asleep.

CHAPTER FOUR

Jennifer is not prepared for what happened next. Exactly at 3:30 p.m., she awakened by a forceful knock on her door. Looking through the window, she saw a black sedan, a Crown Victoria, parked at the curb. "Can I help you?" she said to two men appearing to be in their thirties and dressed in dark business suits.

"Yes!" the taller one explained. "Are you Jennifer Aldrich?"

"What can I do for you?" They both held up what appeared to be FBI badges.

"May we come in? We want to talk to you about a patient at Memorial Hospital." Without responding, she opened the door with little unknown confidence. "I am Special Agent Tilford this is Special Agent Hays. We are investigating an accident and found that you are the one that discovered Mr. David Barr injured alongside the road. We need to know if Mr. Barr was able to talk to you at all. It is important for us to know anything he may have said."

"He told me his name and asked that I call for help. I rode to the hospital in the ambulance with him. He never spoke again. What is this about?"

Handing her a card, he said, "Please call either of us if you have a recollection of anything at all. We may be in touch with you again.

Thank you for your time." With this, they were abruptly gone.

The next day, Monday, she is back on schedule at Memorial and reports for duty at 7:00 a.m. She decided to go in a little early and check on one patient's progress. She is acquainted with the registered nurse on duty at the ICU desk, Sylvia Rymarz, a short stocky woman in her late forties, known to be efficient and conscientious. "Sylvia, how is David Barr doing?"

"He is not awake yet; however, his vitals are improving. No one on the floor knows why, but a plainclothesman is guarding his very bed. They come in shifts. We don't know if they are protecting him or here to see that he doesn't escape."

"What about his mother?"

"Mrs. Barr went home yesterday afternoon, saying very little except the fact that she will return today and to call if there is any change. I understand you are the one who found him."

"Yes, it is hard to say when he would have been discovered if I had gone my regular jogging route."

"His family should be grateful to you."

"I must get to the OR, thanks for the update."

CHAPTER FIVE

It is a grueling day. She assisted in three hip replacements, a laparoscopy, and an appendectomy. The next day promised to be better. Mrs. Barr was at her son's bedside when Jennifer decided to check in on him before returning home.

"Hello, Mrs. Barr, I just wanted to check on David's progress. How are you holding up?"

"I guess okay after getting over the initial shock of seeing David in such a state. I depend upon him so much, although he lives in Washington. He came home for a brief visit. I have not had a chance to thank you for all you have done for us. I dread to think what would have happened to my son if you had not come along."

During the years her son stayed away after graduating from Yale, David called his mother frequently, but concentrated on additional studies and did not return home. He consumed himself studying to further his education, which seemed to ease the pain of having not forgiven himself for resenting his father. He vowed that whatever it took, he would find who killed him and why.

After David had graduated from Jason Academy, a magnet high school for young people, his father insisted he take required subjects in college to enter medical school and ultimately follow his example.

Dr. Barr's only child became a hell-raiser after graduating high school and in total defiance of his father. His mother, sympathetic and more approachable, reluctantly sided with her husband.

Jason Academy, donated to the community by Anderson Baker, a successful retired developer whose son, Jason, died of an overdose when visiting his cousins in Miami ten years before, is a relatively small school operated by the Pioneers. The Pioneers, of which Anderson Baker is a charter member, are select groups of businessmen who formed together to provide extensive education for those fitting requirements and having incentives to enroll in the school. The academy offers scholarships to those qualified but unable to meet total tuition. The academy houses 115 students from out of the vicinity and accommodates 295 in classrooms. Students are expected to participate in sports at Jason Academy. Basketball, tennis, and chess are most prevalent. Drugs, alcohol, and even smoking, are not tolerated. This is to be a school of highly academically skilled students with exceptional goals preparing them for college.

It was David's lifestyle after graduating Jason that prompted an extensive background check by Detective Raymore. This revealed an obvious resentment of his paternal parent, ultimately leading authorities to investigate the son of such a prominent, well respected plastic surgeon murdered at his home. Dr. Barr was a pillar of the community.

Fortunately, four young people came forward immediately to tell Detective Raymore, the lead investigator, that David had spent the night before and the day of the murder with them playing basketball and drinking beer twenty-five miles from his home. They had bought beer from a nearby roadhouse, which was confirmed by the club owner.

For one year after his father's murder, David took a non-productive sabbatical, after which he and his mother decided it was time for him to return to college. After being cleared of any involvement in his father's death and after a few brief therapy sessions with a noted psychologist, he began to forgive himself for not being home to protect his father from harm.

Mrs. Barr confided in Jennifer and confessed she had not known David's exact reason for not returning home, but felt he is on a mission and possibly preparing to investigate his father's death. He continually asked her to keep faith and to trust him, and although it may not be of her choice entirely in the medical field, he is pursuing an education as she had hoped, and she should not worry.

After receiving a law degree from Yale, his obsession led him to study criminology. He went to Washington and learned everything he could about profiling and forensic science. After all these degrees under his belt, David was approached by several law enforcement agencies, and accepted an impressive position heading the criminal investigation division with the FBI. His mother attended his appointment with pride.

CHAPTER SIX

The next morning as she is about to put her head in and exchange pleasantries with the recovering David out of respect for his mother, Jennifer noticed two men standing at his bedside. Although they had their backs to her, one of them is aware of the door leading into David's room. He waved to her as if to say, "This is a private conversation."

At 4:00 p.m., she left the hospital after an exhaustive day in the OR. The surgery on a ten-year-old male having severe back trauma after falling off a horse had taken five hours. His spinal cord appeared severed. Thankfully, that was not the case. Jonathon Miller expected to make a full recovery, thanks to a young neurosurgeon by the name of Abraham Bharne (pronounced Barney), called in from Miami's Mount Sinai Hospital. Jonathon's parents, Karen and Jesse Miller, are a prominent couple in the area and prepared to spare no expense. Jesse, a tax attorney, is also a member of the Pioneers.

Dr. Bharne is most impressive; his hands are that of an artist creating his most important sculpture. He led the team of surgeons with the confidence of a conductor of symphonies. His precision and concentration is notably admired. He stands out from the rest by his calf-high white boots. His dark hair is obvious, although covered by a colorful scarf. His eyes are a serious deep brown, half-mooned by thick black brows.

The next morning, Jennifer, our young hero, called by the hospital staff and by members of her neighborhood, read a most impressive and brief outline of her rescue of the son of a prominent family in the local newspaper. She is off duty and says aloud to herself, "What a restful day this is going to be." After she took Fox for a walk, Jennifer picked up the latest book from her favorite author, John Grisham, and decided to relax on her patio. Her patio, located in the cul-de-sac, is framed by five red azalea shrubs. She has ample privacy. There are hanging baskets of flowers outlining the glass French doors. A fresh scent of hyacinth is forever present. The setting is quite picturesque, anchored by three dogwood trees located in the nearby courtyard, one pink and two white. This is her favorite place to be when weather permits. A subliminal tape, faintly heard from her CD player, adds to the tranquility.

Jennifer's neighbors include Klara Weiszman, a seventy-year-old Holocaust survivor. This special lady, of whom she has become very fond, has short blonde hair, twinkling blue eyes, a smooth tanned complexion, and claims to be Klara with a *k*. Born in Budapest, Ms. Klara rarely speaks of experiences before escaping to America as a young girl. Her memories are too painful. Ms. Klara is Jennifer's favorite neighbor and has become a good friend.

Her newest neighbors are Trudy and Anthony Panachek, both seeming to be in their thirties. Tony is a physical therapist, slight in stature, a quiet, passive individual who seemingly is subservient to his aggressive mate. Trudy is an executive with a local telephone service. She is an attractive brunette with very dark eyes, well dressed, and a self-appointed authority on just about everything. She is disgustingly articulate and usually heard to become argumentative toward Anthony.

CHAPTER SEVEN

Jennifer had just started the third chapter of her book when she was interrupted by the telephone. "Hello, Ms. Aldrich?"

"Yes!"

"This is Dr. Bharne."

Thinking this has to be a call to come back to the hospital, she replies, "Yes, Dr. Bharne, little Jonathon hasn't gotten worse, has he?"

"No! Quite the contrary—he is a strong-willed lad and recovering well. The nursing staff was kind enough to give me your number. I hope you don't mind. I just wanted to commend you for your excellent assistance in the OR."

"Thank you, Doctor. This is quite a compliment. Your reputation of being the best of the best preceded you, only to be confirmed by your presence. We are all humbled."

"Thank you, Ms. Aldrich, you are most kind. If you decide at any time to leave Memorial, I will put in a word for you at Sinai."

"Thank you, Doctor, have a safe and pleasant trip back."

"Goodbye." The conversation was professional, but she detected something personal in his voice. This brought a smile to her face.

CHAPTER EIGHT

Several days had passed since Jennifer found David at the side of the road. He is out of intensive care and expected to make a full recovery. His mother visits once a day, sometimes twice, and has become friendly with the nurse who saved his life.

Jennifer entered David's room after being summoned by his mother. "I would like to thank you properly for saving my life; I am sorry if I have seemed so aloof at times. I appreciate you being so kind to my mother."

"You are quite welcome. Your mother is very easy to be kind to."

"I will be leaving the hospital soon, and after I have a chance to recuperate, I would like to invite you to dinner."

"Why, yes, Mr. Barr, that would be lovely, but not necessary."

"Nonetheless, I will appreciate having an opportunity to chat with you and get to know you better. I will be in touch."

"Thank you, Mr. Barr. I look forward to hearing from you." With this curious thought diminishing, Jennifer excused herself and prepared to leave for home.

The next few days are uneventful for Jennifer. David is discharged from the hospital. Her schedule in the OR is pretty much routine, an occasional knee or hip replacement, and a few scheduled tonsillectomies.

Just when her life seemed to appear relatively normal again after her notoriety, Jennifer received a visit from one of the mysterious strangers she had seen visiting David Barr. The hospital administrator, Mark Powers, called her into his private office before leaving the two of them alone.

Chapter Nine

"Ms. Aldrich, it is nice to see you again. I apologize for the interruption." Jennifer remembered Special Agent Hays from when he and Agent Tilford visited her home. "I will get right to the point. We have reason to believe that Mr. Barr is in extreme danger. Evidence has indicated the accident was an attempt on his life."

"Oh?"

"I am not at liberty to discuss details, but will tell you there is a possibility the assailant or assailants believe you may have seen something or heard David say something that could become incriminating to them. We feel we must take you into our confidence. Mr. Powers assured us you are trustworthy, and we must ask that you not discuss any conversation we have, with him or with anyone."

"I understand, but why would you believe I could be involved? All I did was see a man in trouble and sought help."

"Someone has bugged your phone."

"Am I under surveillance by the FBI?"

"Yes, and by an unknown. We may need your help, but it is strictly voluntary on your part. You will receive the best protection we can offer." With this said, Jennifer relaxes with a long sigh and pause. Hesitantly, she agrees to do what she can. "Thank you, the next time we meet, it will be more discreet. In the meantime, try to go about your life as usual and talk to no one about our meeting. Again, thank you."

When assuming her duties, she comes across Mark Powers, who looked at her inquisitively. "Is everything all right?"

"Yes, thank you." Mark is dedicated to his job and even more to his wife and two young children. Mark is also professional enough not ask any more questions.

Ten days have passed since her conversation with Agent Hays when she received a note from David Barr delivered by Mrs. Barr's chauffeur. The note is an invitation to dinner at the Barr residence. Instructions ask her to call only with regrets. Otherwise, a car, driven by the same chauffeur, will arrive for her at 6:00 p.m. on the following Sunday. Jennifer realizes her life is turning into a strange sort of mystery.

CHAPTER TEN

Deciding to go about her days as normally as possible, she realized it had been a few days since she noticed Ms. Klara walking Ginger, the white Maltese her son had given her three years earlier. The little dog has become a great companion to Ms. Klara and, as she likes to think, a wonderful watchdog.

Ms. Klara, who is usually dressed in a matching outfit with her blonde hair in place and makeup complimenting her tanned face, came to the door in her robe. She explained she is recuperating from the flu and Sammy, the twelve-year-old grandson of nearby friends from Budapest, is caring for Ginger. "Why didn't you call me? What can I do for you?"

"Nothing, dear, you are an angel, but I am much better now." Not satisfied with this after using her stethoscope to check her heart, taking her pulse, and realizing the weakened condition her special neighbor is in, Jennifer insisted on calling Dr. Kleinman.

"Just as a precaution," she explained. Dr. Kleinman is happy to see his favorite patient and without hesitation offered to wait for them to arrive before leaving his office for the day. The doctor, a widower beyond retirement age, seemed to have a special interest in Ms. Klara, although Ms. Klara denies this.

After a routine examination of his patient, Dr. Kleinman emerged to the waiting room. "I want to send Klara to the hospital for some tests.

Will you accompany her?"

"Yes, of course."

"I will call with orders for blood work and an EKG. I want to see what has her in this weakened condition. Try to get her there this evening. She will, however, give you a little song and dance about having the flu and try to get out of going. Be insistent."

After getting Ms. Klara settled comfortably in the hospital and promising to see her in the morning, Jennifer returned home to receive an unexpected phone call and is taken totally off guard to hear Dr. Bharne's voice. He has a patient to see in Macon, an elderly man with a perforated disc that requires evaluation before surgery can be an option. "I will come right to the point," he told her. "I would like to see you. I will arrive in Macon on Thursday and would like to take you to dinner on Friday, your choice of restaurants."

"Dr. Bharne, are you asking me for a date?"

"Absolutely, what do you say?"

"Well, yes! I would love to have dinner with you."

"Good, I will rent a car and be at your place by 7:00 Friday afternoon. By the way, my first name is Abraham, but I am called Rab." After giving directions to her home, Jennifer amused herself by hashing over all that changed her life within the past few weeks. Two years have passed since her fifteen-month romance failed with Alan Fitzgerald, a former patient. Alan had tried to hide a drinking problem and became abusive when confronted. She finds herself looking forward to a date with Dr. Bharne. Today is Saturday and she has a few days left before deciding what to wear.

That morning, Jennifer called Dr. Kleinman to receive good news about Ms. Klara, who is recuperating from an iron deficiency and low blood pressure. "She should be fine with a little rest and medication," he told her. After jogging with Fox, Jennifer decided it was time to start thinking about what to wear to the Barrs' that evening.

Chapter Eleven

She thought of Dr. Barr and his reputation. She remembered meeting him on several occasions when she and her mother visited from Ohio. She remembered playing on the floor in his office. Her mother, who interned at Memorial, was a dermatologist who knew Dr. Barr on a professional level. After her mother's death, he became a good friend and mentor.

Dr. Barr, although living in a small community, became a world-renowned plastic surgeon sought frequently by many patients from large cities.

He provided his patients, most of them wealthy and some famous, with a recuperation facility that he designed and built near the Ocmulgee River. The building is a one-floor construction with seven two-room suites that include a luxury bedroom and living room, each with a patio complete with two lounge chairs and an umbrella table overlooking the Ocmulgee River through a garden of azaleas and perfectly manicured shrubs. The facility provides the latest necessary hospital equipment, nurses as needed, as well as a chef and a dietician. Patients usually stay anywhere from two to eight weeks, depending upon recovery. It is a safe haven, having the security of a large gated fence and twenty-four-hour surveillance by a monitor and guard when occupied. It is indeed a tranquil setting and worth the price tag for those who can manage the cost. Other doctors have privileges at this medical vacation spot, affectionately called the azalea farm by residents. Since Dr. Barr's premature death, his widow donated the building, renamed Avery Hall, to Memorial Hospital to continue as a rehabilitation facility.

Chapter Twelve

Jennifer chose to wear her blonde shoulder-length hair down. She always wears her hair up and back at the hospital when on duty. She looked stunning in a pink satin blouse and matching raw silk pants when the chauffeur-driven car pulled up at exactly 6:00 p.m. Hans, the chauffeur, escorted her from her front door to the car and directed her to join David in the back seat. "Hello, thank you for joining us."

"Hello, Mr. Barr, how are you feeling?"

"Very well, thank you, I get stronger every day. Please, call me David."

It is a ten-minute drive to the Barr estate, a beautifully restored Victorian mansion built in the late 1800s. Mrs. Barr greeted them inside the study, which at a glance was tastefully decorated with two dark red couches facing each other in front of a fireplace, a sofa table behind each. Family pictures were tastefully placed on the mantel. Three walls housed dark cherry wood shelving from chair height to ceiling, containing systematically arranged collections of books for reading and reference.

Mrs. Barr promptly offered drinks. She was dressed in an informal emerald green gown and looked to be the perfect hostess. David had on a white long-sleeved shirt with a pair of designer jeans and tan mephisto loafers. He is just under six feet, she thought to herself, noticing how good he looked out of the hospital bed. She knew from his hospital chart that he is five years older than she. It is apparent from the family pictures in the study that he is quite a bit thinner since the accident. His hair is blonde, about the same color as hers. She could not help but think he must be popular among his friends, especially the ladies.

After a glass of chardonnay served at the dining table, dinner consisted of a light salad prepared by the cook. Spinach, herbs, mandarin oranges, and feta cheese were the main ingredients. A rack of lamb, like none she had ever tasted, was served along with baked yams and steamed asparagus. It was a wonderful dinner, complimented by a light raspberry sorbet for the finality.

With coffee served in the study after dinner, Mrs. Barr excused herself for the evening. "David will see you home, Jennifer, thank you for your company."

"Mrs. Barr," Jennifer said, taking her hand, "thank you so much for such a delightful meal and pleasant evening. Your cook is indeed a jewel."

"You are very welcome." David kisses his mother on the cheek.

"Goodnight, Mother, pleasant dreams."

"Goodnight, son. Goodnight, Jennifer."

Chapter Thirteen

After she and David exchanged comments about the weather and his recovery, he asked, "How long have you been a nurse at Memorial?"

"This is my third year. I tried private duty for a while."

"Where did you go to school?"

"In Columbus, Ohio, through my teen years, and then my mother and I moved to Ft. Meyers, Florida. She was a dermatologist and there were more opportunities for her there. I graduated from the University of Miami and came here to pursue a nursing career. It was my mother's wish. She knew people here and wanted me to be safe. Your father befriended me and often asked about my grades."

"Where were you born?"

"In Columbus—you ask a lot of questions."

"I'm sorry, I just feel that our paths have crossed before. How did your mother die?"

"She was struck by a driver that seemingly was drunk, but his lawyer proved that it was a reaction from medication that made him pass out."

"What about your father?"

"My father was never a part of my life. When I was eleven years old, Mother told me that my father was a married man that she had known only briefly. I discovered in later years after Mother's death that he had died when

27

Iraqi forces stormed a number of diplomatic missions in Kuwait City. He was an English businessman working for the American government. The information did not include the name of a wife or children."

"When did your mother's accident occur?"

"Before I graduated from college. What about your life, what do you do? I know you live in Washington." She is getting comfortable asking him questions by now and is very much at ease with him.

"I work for the government." He didn't seem to want to elaborate on anything further. "I look for the bad guys. Look, Jen." She hadn't been called Jen since her mother died. "I know that a couple of agents have been in contact with you. I want you to know you can trust them. I am so sorry that by helping me you put yourself in jeopardy. I hope this situation will be over soon. In the meantime, go about your business as usual and if you see or hear anything suspicious at all, please contact Hays, Tilford, or myself. If I need to contact you about anything other than personal matters, I will contact you at work or through Hans."

"David, what do you expect to happen?"

"I expect the unexpected. There may be another attempt on my life. Not to worry, the security around me is quite elaborate. If you are ready, I will take you home. I understand you have a full schedule tomorrow."

"You know my schedule?"

"Yes, I am one of your protectors. There is no need to panic; we do not take unnecessary chances."

Upon taking her home, David kisses her on the cheek and waits for Hans, a German immigrant obviously quite devoted to the Barr family, to walk her to the door. "I will stay in contact with you, Jen."

"Thank you, David."

Jennifer felt more comfortable having her dog, Fox, in her room at night. Fox barks relentlessly at the least noise until quieted by his master.

CHAPTER FOURTEEN

The next day, Monday morning, Ms. Klara was released from the hospital. Dr. Kleinman, himself, took her home. And he is not interested? After her busy day at the hospital, Jennifer took some homemade soup to Ms. Klara, chatted for a while and started to leave when she heard Fox barking. Looking out the window, she noticed someone running from her patio. "What is it, dear?" asked Ms. Klara.

"Oh nothing, he probably saw a squirrel. I will check on you tomorrow." She left and immediately called Agent Hays from her cell phone. He was at her door in minutes.

"You didn't go in, did you?"

"No, I waited for you like you asked." Hays searched the grounds and for forced entry before they entered the condo. Nothing seemed to be out of place other than a small piece of paper placed inside the screen on the patio. Hays picked it up gently and read it aloud: "*Find your father's identity and you will know why your mother was killed.*"

"What about your mother? How was she killed?"

"It was years ago when I was in school, supposedly by an overmedicated driver. He was never prosecuted. I never knew my father. My mother was vague other than telling me he was a married man. What does all this mean?"

"I don't know, but we will find out. Did you see the person at all that left your patio?"

"Just his back as he ran. He had on a dark cap and navy jacket."

"The person that left this note is just a messenger. He probably means you no harm. We will have the paper analyzed and checked for prints and put twenty-four-hour surveillance on your home until we check thoroughly."

"Thank you. I was devastated losing my mother, and this opens up all the memories."

"I promise we will not stop until we resolve all this. Just stay calm; it may all be a hoax. I will report this to Agent Barr."

"Agent Barr—is David Barr part of the FBI?"

"He is my superior."

CHAPTER FIFTEEN

The next few days proved to be without incident for Jennifer. The only evidence of surveillance was a utility truck parked up the block in a lot under construction.

David ordered a background on Jennifer's mother, Dr. Janelle Aldrich, to include Jennifer's birth certificate. The father is listed as Winston Gates, businessman. Dr. Aldrich was well respected in her field and by the few acquaintances she had outside her practice. Her personal life is a mystery, as is Winston Gates.

A more extensive investigation was put into place. Records of her patients revealed that she and Dr. Barr treated some of the same patients. This is not uncommon, as skin treatment often followed plastic surgery and Dr. Aldrich was active at Memorial during that time. Two patients stood out among the rest. One had the last name of Salerno and the other, Donetti. Both gave Las Vegas addresses, which proved to be bogus. These two names were initially investigated by Detective Raymore in the death of Dr. Barr, but the case went cold without further evidence. Dr. Aldrich was killed two years before Dr. Barr's body was discovered.

Thursday evening, Jennifer received a call from Rab confirming their date for Friday. She gave directions to her home and suggested going to Saunders restaurant, which was well known for wonderful seafood dishes. The restaurant has a relaxing atmosphere but she wondered how she can be herself with everything that has happened lately.

Expecting that he would be punctual, she prepared herself in advance. To compliment her green eyes, she chose a lime silk sleeveless blouse tied at the waist and white designer pants. Although only five feet four inches tall, she looked like a fashion model after donning four-inch white pumps. Her crystal earrings were the same color of green as her blouse. It was obvious by his expression that Rab was impressed by what he saw when arriving exactly at 7:00 p.m. as promised. He made an indelible appearance with a sense of propriety and refinement in an ecru raw silk blazer, open shirt, and light tan trousers. They arrived at the restaurant in an off-white Lincoln Town Car, which he rented in Macon. The weather is pleasant enough for the sunroof to be open with a full view of a half moon and partly cloudy sky.

Dinner consisted of a small caesar salad, twice-baked potato, and lobster tail, complimented by a recommended white chardonnay. Although the dinner was delightful, Jennifer was concentrating on what a good conversationalist her companion is and how much she is enjoying his company. The two of them laughed together and exchanged knowledge of individual patients, current political issues, and their positions in the job force. This was truly a delightful evening and obviously enjoyed by both. All her anxieties seemed to vanish for the present.

Not until Rab was tipping the valet did she notice the familiar car that had been following them. The two agents were easily recognized by Jennifer who brought her back to the realization of the dangers still lurking.

Rab walked her to the front door of her condo, and kissed her lightly and unassumingly, with the promise of calling in the future. They both exchanged wonderful thoughts of the evening and he drove away. She wondered if she would hear from him again. The car with Agents Tilford and Hays is parked conspicuously at the end of the block, which brought her back to the current events and an element of fear.

CHAPTER SIXTEEN

Jennifer is awakened early Saturday morning before daybreak by the sound of sirens. An ambulance and two patrol cars were stopped on her street in front her cul-de-sac. Immediately, she thought of Ms. Klara. Four policemen, with guns drawn, ran to the condo occupied by Trudy and Anthony Panachek. By this time, lights were appearing from every unit. A knock at her front door revealed Agent Hays, who came to tell her what had occurred. "Jennifer, there has been a double homicide at one of your neighbors'. A 911 call came in at 3:40 a.m. from a Trudy Panachek. Both she and Anthony Panachek had been stabbed and died before anyone could get there. It looked like an intruder was waiting for them when they arrived home."

"Oh my God! Was it robbery? Where were you? I thought you people were posted out front."

"We were out front watching every one of your entrances. There was not a threat to anyone else in the area that we are aware of. The police found that one of the back bedroom windows of the condo had been tampered with. Also, evidence had shown that the intruder or intruders were staying in the condo while the Panacheks were out of town." Two hours after the crime scene investigators arrived, the Panacheks were removed by ambulance. The neighbors were devastated and all gathered together to express horror and concern.

"Why has this happened? Is it connected to the Barrs?"

"It is too early to assume anything, Jennifer. Everyone in the neighborhood will be interviewed as to what they have seen. Please try to remain calm."

"Remain calm? I am under surveillance because of a murder investigation, which happened several years ago; I may be in harm by what I don't know. My neighbors are being murdered. I can't have a decent date without the FBI lurking over my shoulder."

"Jennifer, believe me, I understand and we will do everything possible to get to the bottom of this."

David Barr arrived before the bodies were removed, for a briefing with Agent Hays. "Jennifer, I promise you we will find out why and who did this to your neighbors. Right now the only visible evidence is a partial shoe print left near Mr. Panachek's body and a cutting tool outside the bedroom window. It does not appear to be a robbery, but it is too early to tell for sure."

"David, I am frightened."

"I know, Jen, which is why I want you to stay at another location for a while."

"Where? I can't leave my home. My dog is here. My neighbors are frightened. Some of them need to know that I am here to be of support to them."

"Another alternative is for us to have someone move into your spare room temporarily. Someone trained to have a watchful eye on anything suspicious."

"I don't know, David. I will think about it."

CHAPTER SEVENTEEN

"In the meantime, Jen, I want to get together with you on another matter. I have been investigating the name identified as your father on your birth certificate. This might come as a complete shock to you, but we have reason to believe the name to be bogus."

"Oh my God! What else is going to happen?"

"I want you to think back to anything you can come up with that your mother may have told you or you may have seen or heard during your childhood that can help. Something you may think is insignificant could be the key to what we need. Will you do that?"

"David," she said, with tears in her eyes, "this is overwhelming right now."

"I know." Taking her in his arms, he said, "I didn't like telling you like this, but we are forced to speed up our investigation and look for a tie-in.

"We are about to wind up here for the time being. There will be a detail standing guard until I decide how best you will be protected. Take this cell phone number. You can reach me twenty-four hours a day." With this said, David kisses her forehead. "Stay strong; you will hear from me very soon." Jennifer, suddenly realizing closeness to David Barr, starts to feel relaxed and safe in his presence.

"Thank you, David."

After a brief visit with Ms. Klara and some of the other neighbors who are still in shock, Jennifer prepares to go to work when the phone rings. "Hello, Ms. Aldrich, this is Mark Powers; I just heard what happened in your neighborhood and I want you to take the day off. This has got to be horrific for you. I have contacted Sylvia Rymarz to schedule a replacement for you for a couple of days."

"Oh! Thank you, Mr. Powers. I do need to have a little time. I really appreciate your concern."

The day is filled with fear and anxiety for all the residents of her cul-de-sac. There are so many questions. She spent a good time with Ms. Klara, trying to convince her that what happened would not be repeated.

"Ms. Klara, if Ginger barks at anything you think is suspicious, call me immediately and I will call the authorities. No matter what time it is."

"Thank you, Jennifer, I am so frightened. This reminds me of dangerous times before coming to America."

Chapter Eighteen

At 5:30 p.m., David arrived at the crime scene, accompanied by a woman who looked to be in her middle thirties. "Jen, this is Detective Marsha Benning. I want her to stay with you for a few nights. Marsha is a ten-year veteran with the special units force in Macon. She has a lot of experience and I think the two of you will get along just fine."

"How do you do, Ms. Aldrich? I know this is hard for you and I will do my best not to be too much of an intruder."

"Thank you, Detective, I trust David to do what is best."

"Please, call me Marsha."

"I will leave you two ladies to get acquainted and see you tomorrow." He kisses Jen on the cheek and departs.

After offering Marsha something to eat, the two watched TV for about an hour before Jennifer excused herself to retire. Marsha, a thirty-five-year-old attractive five-foot-six Latina, made friends with Fox before making herself at home in the guest room, but stayed awake most of the night fully dressed with her weapon by her side.

In the morning, David called to invite Jen to lunch, which she excitedly accepted. David and his chauffeur, Special Agent Hays, picked her up at 11:30 as promised and drove to a popular French café in the center of town. Agent Hays positioned himself outside the café to keep a watchful eye while the two enjoyed a delightful lunch consisting of a light chicken soup with homemade noodles and small hearts of palm salads. Jennifer felt as though they were becoming fast friends.

David, having positioned himself to have a full view of the restaurant, starts a casual conversation. "Jen, have you thought about anything else we discussed concerning what your mother told you over the years or what you have heard about your father?"

"My memories are not that good because Mother seemed not to want to complicate his life by taking a chance of his wife finding out about a child. I believe your father knew my father well, because I remember occasions when I was a small child, visiting here with my mother, and Dr. Barr came by our hotel, had lunch with us, and told me that my father loved me very much. We also visited Dr. Barr's office several times. He said that he would be in touch with him and tell him how I had grown. It became obvious to me in later years that my mother and your father shared a mutual respect."

"What about other occasions?"

"When I graduated with honors from Miami University and moved here to go to nursing school. Your father attended my graduation and was instrumental in finding proper housing for me. He actually seemed to take me under his wing. He said many times that my mother was not only a colleague of his, but a great friendship that he would always cherish. He also told me that since neither parent was around for me, he wanted me to come to him with any problems or uncertainties I may have about school, etc. At that time I asked him to tell me all he knew about my father. All he would say was that he was a good person who cared for my mother very much, but could not leave his family, which he also loved. My father evidently was in close contact with Dr. Barr and was kept aware of my early childhood. I, too, lost a good friend and mentor when your father was killed. He used to tell me about his son, David. He was so proud of you."

CHAPTER NINETEEN

Just then, Agent Hays appeared at the table and insisted they leave immediately. Two suspicious men had gone to the back of the café and were trying to gain entrance through the kitchen by bribing a bus boy. The local authorities had been called and were on the way.

Just as the sirens were nearing the street, Agent Tilford pulled up in another car and whisked the two away, screeching around the corner. "Jen, it is me that they are after. We are getting close to solving my father's murder, and some people don't want it solved."

Upon reaching Jennifer's home, David went inside to await Hays, while Tilford guarded the perimeter. About an hour later, Hays arrived with news about the would-be intruders. "David, the two suspects have been detained. They won't say much, but both were armed. Their identification is being processed."

"Thanks, Matt." Matthew Hays has been a subordinate of David's for a number of years, although they have remained close friends.

It is 10:00 a.m. the next morning when Jennifer answered the phone to hear Rab's voice. "Hello, Jennifer, I hope I haven't caught you at a bad time."

"No, not at all, it's good to hear from you. How are you?"

"I have been pretty busy, but ready to take a few days off. Do you think you could take a long weekend and visit Miami? I would like to show you around the hospital."

"I don't know, Rab; a lot has happened in my neighborhood lately. Two of my neighbors have been killed."

"Oh no! I am very sorry to hear that. Was it an accident?"

Jennifer did not want to say much on the phone. "I really don't know what the details are as yet."

"It sounds as if you could stand a break. If you think you can make it, I will reserve a room for you at the Eden Roc Hotel on Miami Beach."

"It sounds wonderful. May I call you back after I check out a few things?"

"Yes, of course." He gives her his cell phone number. "Please leave a message if I am unable to answer."

When the conversation was over, Marsha walked into the room to see an obvious glow on Jennifer's face and smiled. "Marsha, may I confide in you about a personal matter?"

"From the expression on your face, it must be a happy matter."

"I have been invited away for the weekend by someone whom I respect. He is a doctor in Miami with whom I have had one dinner date. I am not sure if he is interested in me or if he is courting me as a potential employee for his hospital."

"What are the accommodation arrangements?"

"He has offered to put me up in a hotel near the hospital."

"Jennifer, I think it sounds wonderful and it would be good for you to get away. I can plan to stay here and keep an eye on things. I have become quite attached to Fox. Why don't you talk it over with Agent Barr?"

"Thank you, Marsha, I will."

When David arrived that afternoon to update Marsha and Jennifer about the two arrested the day before at the restaurant, he had some startling news. Agent John Tilford is missing from his hotel room. The room had been ransacked to look like a robbery and there were signs of a struggle. Tilford had been with the bureau for a short time and had proven to be a credit to the organization. His expertise has been investigating notable crime figures. "An intensive investigation is in progress and we are praying for his safe return. There are a couple of leads that we are working on.

"The two in custody have been linked to crime figures in Chicago, but are reluctant to cooperate. However, the pressure on them has intensified since Tilford's disappearance. Two hotel clerks have given us a description of three suspicious men who had gone up the elevator the morning of his disappearance. I have contacted the bureau. They will be sending someone down to help in this investigation."

"Who would be so brazen as to kidnap an FBI agent, and why?"

"Jen, the people behind this are not intimidated easily. The ones they hire to do their dirty work are no more than unsophisticated hoods that will make mistakes. They either want to find out what we know or to slow down our investigation. We are more equipped and have enough manpower to outsmart the best of criminals. I do want you to go to another location for a short time. I cannot take a chance on them using you for a pawn."

" David, I have been invited by a friend to go to Miami for a long weekend. Is this a bad time?"

"No, actually, this is a very good time. I will need details of your whereabouts at all times and names of the people you will be in contact with."

Chapter Twenty

It is 10:50 a.m. on Thursday when Delta Flight 1060 landed at Miami International Airport. As she deplaned, Jennifer glanced into the waiting gallery when her eye focused on a sign which read *Jennifer with the Beautiful Green Eyes.* As she saw Rab peeking from behind the sign with a smile larger than life, she began to feel comfortable with the situation. He is wearing a chocolate-colored short-sleeve shirt opened at the neck, light tan trousers, and white shoes with no socks.

"Rab, you are a little crazy."

"We have just enough time to get you checked in before I take you to lunch."

"That sounds wonderful." She is delighted to discover that besides his professionalism and Mediterranean good looks, he has a sense of humor and is very down-to-earth. She is very impressed with the two-room suite he reserved for her overlooking the ocean from the fifth floor. The balcony, complete with lounge chairs, wrapped around two sides of the suite with access through sliding glass doors from the living room as well as from the bedroom. The room with one king-sized bed is decorated in pale pinks and yellows, characteristic of Florida hues.

While she freshened up in the bedroom, Rab filled two long-stemmed glasses with champagne chilling in a bucket on the bar next to a bowl of strawberries.

Jennifer came out of the bedroom, looking delightfully fresh in a pair of white dress shorts, low white heels, and a silk yellow blouse. "Jennifer, I thought you looked good before, but…"

"Thank you, Rab."

"You aren't allergic to strawberries, are you?"

"No, I love strawberries." He dropped a strawberry in her glass of champagne and the two talked about what he planned for her visit. Lunch was a little drive away, but very pleasant at the Bal Harbour shopping center. After lunch, they walked through the shopping center, looking at all the shops.

"I don't want to wear you out on your first day here. Therefore, I am going to take you back to the hotel and let you rest until I pick you up for dinner this evening. By the way, dinner is casual; we will be on the water."

Back at the hotel, Rab walked her to the elevator, leaving after a peck on the cheek and a promise to pick her up at 7:00 p.m. Jennifer is grateful to have the time to walk around the hotel area and lounge by the pool.

She took the time to phone David as he requested. Her first question is about Agent Tilford. "No, Jen, we don't have him yet, but are confident and have reason to be hopeful. Now, what do you know about this Dr. Bharne?" He was starting to sound like either a jealous suitor or an overly cautious lawman.

"I know he is well respected in the medical field and he has treated me with the utmost kindness and respect."

"I'm sorry, I don't mean to pry into your personal relationships. I just want you to be safe."

"I do appreciate your concern, David, but I don't feel threatened here."

"Good, just have a relaxing time and please stay in touch."

Rab arrived exactly at 7:00 p.m. He appeared quite handsomely athletic in a pair of khaki shorts and a navy sport shirt. Jennifer wore white shorts with a pale pink cotton blouse. She promptly changed shoes to sneakers after observing his deck shoes. He entertained her on a small private yacht docked behind his home on Star Island. The craft, piloted by Captain Mel Chavez, was scheduled for a short cruise after dinner. The candlelight meal included snow crabs, spinach salad, and a delightful steamed vegetable tray complimented by a bottle of Clos Du Bois chardonnay, all prepared and served by Marcilene, whom Rab described as "my favorite dietician; she watches my cholesterol three days a week. The other four days I'm in charge and sneak in a steak or two."

The couple enjoyed a wonderful evening on the water, after which he took her on a tour of his home. The five-bedroom two-story luxurious estate described as having been used by a former Mexican revolutionary leader, Doroteo Arango, in the late 1800s, is lavishly furnished, dominating a masculine touch. Rab proudly admitted to having a big part in choosing the décor.

He indicated that his mother lived in the north wing, a section they did not enter.

"Where is your mother now?"

"She is visiting my brother in London. I would like you to meet her one day. She is quite extraordinary." They relaxed with a night cap at the outside bar, gazing at the Miami skyline across the water, before Rab drove her back to the Eden Roc. It is a delightful evening and one she would not forget.

CHAPTER TWENTY-ONE

The remainder of her visit, Rab remained attentive but always above reproach. They went on a casino cruise one evening and on an air boat ride during an afternoon. He took her on a short tour of Mt. Sinai Hospital, where she was greeted by some of his colleagues, discovering that one in particular, a scrub nurse named Jillian, seemed to be intimidated by her presence. Jennifer wondered if Jillian had been a romantic interest. She seemed to have as much interest in Jennifer as she would have in hoof-and-mouth disease.

Monday morning came all too soon as she prepared to return to what had proven to be a world of turmoil. The phone rang at 6:00 a.m. "Good morning, Jennifer. This is Rab." As if she didn't recognize his slight Mediterranean accent.

"I have an emergency surgery in an hour and will be unable to take you to the airport."

"I will be fine, Rab, and happy to take the shuttle. I cannot thank you enough for this wonderful trip. You are a special person and I value your friendship very much."

"You are most welcome, Jennifer; it is indeed a pleasure. Someday, perhaps, we will be more than friends." This was the first indication, besides telling her he would like her to meet his mother, that he might want to pursue a more romantic interest. Maybe he is not seeking another nurse for his hospital after all. Jennifer, on the other hand, realized she had become quite enamored with him. "I am happy you had a good time, Jennifer. I know you can take the shuttle. However, I have taken the liberty of sending a driver for you. He will arrive at your hotel at 8:00 a.m., which will give you plenty of time for your 10:00 a.m. flight. His name is Raoul and he is quite reliable. Have a pleasant trip. I will be in touch." With this brief conversation over, she did not have time to protest. She continued packing and is waiting in the lobby at 8:00 a.m. when a large Hispanic man approached and asked if she was Ms. Aldrich.

"Yes, I am; you must be Raoul." He didn't seem to have spent much time on the English language, but politely picked up her luggage and gestured for her to follow him to the car. He opened the back door of a black Lincoln Town Car, which appears to be a small private limo used for VIP travelers. The small bar was equipped with bottles of ice water.

David arrived at the airport in Macon early to escort Jennifer home. He had located and rescued Special Agent Tilford after two informants in custody decided to try for a plea bargain and give the names of the three assailants assigned to rough up an FBI agent in order to intimidate David Barr. They knew the agent's whereabouts were probably confined to the hotel. This was the plan.

Nothing else earth-shattering had happened in Jennifer's absence.

Agent Tilford was close to escaping on his own, when he was found bound and gagged in a closet inside an unoccupied room at his hotel. The two grabbed him, tried to gain information from him, and left when they became disappointed.

As a precaution, Marsha is still staying at Jennifer's condo most of the time. Little progress had been made in the Panachek murders. A motive is not obvious.

46

Chapter Twenty-Two

Jennifer's flight arrived ten minutes later than scheduled. David found himself looking forward to seeing her again as he watched the first-class passengers deplane. Twenty minutes later, all the passengers seemed to have left the plane. "Where is Jen?" David immediately checked her itinerary only to find it correct. He called her cell. No answer. He rushed to the security office, flashing his badge, a sick feeling in his gut. His palms were sweaty and shaking.

She was assigned a seat in first class, leaving Miami, but did not check in for the flight. An all points bulletin is quickly issued and a search for Jennifer Aldrich was underway in and around the Miami Airport, including the Eden Roc Hotel. An urgent call put in to Dr. Bharne at Mt. Sinai Hospital brought no immediate response. Dr. Bharne is in surgery and could not be disturbed.

Realizing how attached he had become to Jennifer, David booked the next flight to Miami without hesitation. Three hours later, three Miami FBI agents met David's plane and were ready to assist in any way possible to find the missing woman. Their first stop is Mt. Sinai Hospital. Dr. Abraham Bharne was waiting for them to arrive, not knowing what to think. Jennifer had not elaborated on the situations developing at home since or before the murders of her neighbors.

Seeing Dr. Bharne's shocked expression when David explained some of his fears and why he had them, David was relatively confident that Dr. Bharne was genuinely concerned and had nothing to do with her disappearance.

The next urgency is to locate Raoul. Rab insisted that Raoul is a person of integrity and would not harm anyone. "He is the husband of my cook and very much respected by me and all who know him. He drives for a small independent limo service called Limits." David promptly called the supervisor at Limits, who had not heard from Raoul since that morning. He missed a scheduled pick-up at a downtown office building. According to the owner of Limits, Raoul had never been late, unless because of a traffic problem, and never completely missed a run. The FBI called for an extensive search for the car and for Raoul.

David and one of the local agents, Michael James, headed to the Eden Roc to question anyone who may have seen something. Rab insisted on going with them.

They searched the room she occupied and found nothing out of the ordinary. David requested an interview with everyone on duty that would have come in contact with Jennifer during her stay at the hotel.

The valet remembered seeing her leave the hotel. He was familiar with Raoul and the car which often picks up or delivers passengers along Collins Avenue.

Realizing this is the information needed to know that Jen and Raoul did leave the hotel with no apparent incident, the three men started down the steps to leave. Just then, the concierge ran after them, remembering that a man approached her on the afternoon before, asking her to please check to see if his sister had a reservation in the dining room at any time, as he wanted to surprise her. The sister's name was given as Jennifer Aldrich. The concierge could not confirm any reservation and the man left. He was about fifty years old, dark, with a moustache, and wore out-of-season clothes. "He seemed to be around six feet tall." This is all she could recall. The description was similar to one of the men involved in Agent Tilford's abduction, but that man is in custody.

It is almost midnight and Jennifer, along with Raoul and the car, have been missing since morning. Still there is no trace. David, along with his new acquaintance, Dr. Rab Bharne, is exhausted. Rab insists that David stay at his home, and the two depart from the local agents, who plan to stay on the case all night, extending the search with the information they have. They promise to be in touch with the slightest lead. At 2:00 a.m., David's cell phone rings. The car is identified by a station attendant on Highway 27 through a license plate number. The driver, a dark haired Hispanic, had stopped for gas around 4:00 p.m. No apparent passengers were in the car. The car then headed north. A credit card bearing the name of a woman, Maria Perez, was used.

Chapter Twenty-Three

Morning came not all too soon. Jennifer's picture, along with her chauffeur's picture, is displayed on every major network as well as in the *Miami Herald*. Rab made coffee and located a replacement for himself at the hospital for the next few days. The two of them discussed what might have been overlooked. Rab was blaming himself for not taking her to the airport and David was blaming himself for not keeping surveillance on her in Miami. He explained to Rab that an ongoing investigation about his father's death had involved Jennifer, and the reason is not apparent as yet.

"Her neighbors had been murdered, which leads me to believe there is a connection to Jennifer that she is unaware of. Jennifer saved my life and I will do everything in my power to save hers."

"David, Jennifer has not told me too much of her past, but I get the impression she is worried about who she is and especially who her father was."

"Yes, I know. I am checking out possible candidates from leads we have."

"What about your father? Do you know why he was murdered?"

"He was a prominent plastic surgeon and I believe that to be a significant connection. I'm not at liberty to discuss my findings at this point. However, I feel we are closer."

"Do you mind my asking what your relationship is with Jennifer?"

"No, not at all, as I said, she saved my life when I was left for dead. She stayed in contact with my mother during my recuperation and we seemed to have an instant respect for one another. We have had no romantic or physical contact, if that is what you are asking, although I find her extremely attractive. What about you?"

"I have been around her a minimal time, but ample time to know I would like to know her better. We have a good time together. I love her eyes and how they light up when she laughs. She has a terrific sense of humanity, and I...just want her to be safe."

It is going on noon and they have heard nothing further. Marcilene called for the third time, asking for any news about her husband, Raoul. "I am so sorry, Marcilene, I will call as soon as I hear anything at all."

"Thank you, Dr. Rab, God bless you."

At 3:00 p.m., Agent Michael James called with devastating news. Raoul had been found by a couple of Indian fishermen in the swamp along Route 75 on the way to Ft. Meyers. He had been shot in the head, execution style. The car is still missing, as is Jennifer. "Marcilene will be devastated. I am going over to tell her before she hears it on the news."

"I am so sorry. Rab, I am having a car pick me up to go to Naples. The black limo has been discovered off Route 41 in Naples. When you return, take any calls that may come in for me. I have three agents in Georgia that must stay in touch with me. I have given your number in case I cannot be reached on my cell."

"Yes, of course. We will stay in touch."

CHAPTER TWENTY-FOUR

It is dusk on the second day of her abduction when Jennifer wakes from a deep induced sleep. Her hands are handcuffed to narrow metal posts on a day bed. Her mouth is dry. There are no sheets on the bed. Metal springs are exposed. Nothing else is in the room, with the exception of one faded blue stuffed chair. The wooden floor is bare and there is no air conditioning. The walls are that of a log cabin. She is numb all over and very thirsty. She calls out and a young woman in her twenties, with straggly brown hair, wearing blue jean cut-offs and a red halter top, appears with a bottle of water and a key to unlock the handcuffs. "Who are you and where is this?" The woman does not speak. She points to an adjacent room where Jennifer finds a commode and pedestal wash basin both in need of cleaning. After splashing water on her face to wake herself up, she struggles to get back to sit in the chair. The woman points to the bed, but Jennifer pretends to be too weak to move.

Jennifer pleads, "Please, talk to me. What am I doing here?" The woman decides her captive is too incoherent to cause trouble and leaves the room without restraining her again or making eye contact. She locks the door. Jennifer, shaking uncontrollably, quickly looks for her purse and cell phone. Her luggage is in the room, but it has been ransacked. There is no purse and no phone. There is one small port window that looks out over a lake. A heavy fog threatens to engulf the surroundings.

At 9:00 p.m., Marsha answered the phone in Jennifer's condo. "We have something you want and we are willing to make a trade. Tell Agent Barr we will be in contact." The voice on the other end was determinedly clear with a prominent Italian accent.

"Hello, Dr. Bharne?"

"Yes!"

"This is Agent Marsha Benning; I have information for Special Agent Barr and his cell is out of range. If you hear from him first, please tell him it is urgent."

"Marsha, is it about Jennifer?"

"I believe so, but I am not sure. David will know how to find out."

"I will try to call him also. Thank you, Marsha."

Twenty minutes later, David called Rab after talking to Marsha. "It sounds as if Jennifer has been abducted for a ransom. The person calling claims we have something they want in exchange for what they have. We assume this means Jennifer. This is a good sign so far. It gives me hope she is alive. They want to contact me. Hopefully it will be soon. Keep your hopes up."

"Thanks, David."

In the meantime, Mrs. Barr contacted her son in response to a call from the FBI lab. She knew he was away on a case, but had no idea that her favorite nurse was missing until she turned on the news. "David, it's Mother! What has happened to Jennifer?"

"Mother, are you okay?"

"Yes, but what about you and Jennifer?"

"I promise to bring her home in good shape. It may take a little while, but we have our best people looking for her."

"Oh! David, I am so worried about you."

"Mother, don't be alarmed, but as a precaution, I have called to have a twenty-four-hour watch on your house. I'm sure you will be safe, but you know how we sons like to pamper our mothers. However, I do want you to stay at home until you hear from me. If you need anything, send Hans. I have talked to him and he will be keeping a watch on you until I can. Love you."

"Wait, I have a message from the FBI lab. They have the information you requested."

"Thanks, Mother. Talk to you soon."

It was too late to call the lab. It would have to wait until tomorrow. There are more pressing issues now. "Please, God, keep Jen safe."

Chapter Twenty-Five

"David, this is Marsha. The same person called again. We have a tape of his voice. He wants to talk to you and will call Dr. Bharne's residence at 9:00 a.m. He seems to know the number."

"Thanks, Marsha, I'll head back over there."

Jennifer awakened, terrified, after dozing off continually. There is no sound, indicating she is alone as she unsuccessfully tries to break the glass in the small window with her shoes. Finally she hears two voices, a male and a female. The door is being unlocked as her heart pounds. The same young girl came into the room with a hamburger, apparently from a local fast food chain. The man was not visible. She thought about attempting to overcome the girl, but the man's voice in the other room was intimidating enough to prevent her from trying. She would wait until an opportune time. At least they were keeping her alive, but what has happened to Raoul?

She started to remember a confrontation between two men and Raoul after a green van pulled up alongside the passenger side of the car she was in. One person took her out of the car as the other drove off with her chauffeur. "What do they want?"

She begins to think about Rab and the time they shared the past few days. She wonders how worried David must be when she didn't arrive on the plane. "He is surely looking for me." She shudders, thinking about her neighbors that were slaughtered. "I wonder if Ms. Klara is okay.

"What about my father; who is he? Why did my mother keep things from me? What has happened to Special Agent John Tilford? Has he been killed like the Panacheks?" All these things are reflecting upon her with no obvious solution to any. She tries to listen to the voices in the next room. She heard the woman call the man Hugo. They were speaking to each other in English, but he seemed to be speaking on a phone in Italian. She got down on her hands and knees to look under the door, but could only see shadows. Afraid to be handcuffed again, she decided to be quiet and not cause any disturbance. She listened to every word and finally heard the man say he will be back in an hour. Perhaps she can overpower the woman and escape. "Please, God, help me."

After a briefing with local special agents, David and Agent Michael James started across Alligator Alley to Miami and Rab's house to wait for the 9:00 a.m. call.

CHAPTER TWENTY-SIX

Jennifer Aldrich has been missing for two days. "What do you think they want?"

"I don't know for sure, but I think documents, Mike. I believe it has something to do with records my father may have hidden.

"Sources have informed us that the head of a group of criminals, a Chicago crime family, have elected a new boss by the name of Vinni Peche. It seems Vinni is out to make a name for himself and will do anything to find and murder a person known to be in the witness protection program. Vinni, a slightly built, loud mouthed bully at five foot seven, with the "little man syndrome" has had residences in Chicago, New York, and Miami.

"I believe my father was killed to keep him from giving information wanted by mob members of the Salerno family in Sicily several years ago. I believe also that Jennifer Aldrich's mother, a doctor, was privy to the same information and was killed intentionally. The case went cold and almost forgotten by the mob until Vinni came along. There were a couple attempts on my life, but I believe they now want to keep me alive until they get what they want. I am more worried about those around me. My mother should be safe with the security systems at her home and the extra team we have added to include attack dogs on her property."

"Please help me." Jennifer speaks softly to the woman behind the door. "I have cut my leg on the bed spring." After several calls for help, the woman slowly opened the door to find Jennifer apparently doubled over in pain. When she leaned over, Jennifer jabbed the woman in the stomach with her elbow and then hit her in the face with the heel of her shoe. Stunned, the woman falls to the floor as Jennifer runs out the door instinctively grabbing a cell phone off the table on the way. Her heart beats fast as she runs through a dense wooded area. A lot of water around tells her this is the denizens of a most dangerous spot. Just as she paused to take a breath, she saw headlights headed for the cabin she had left. As she is forcing herself through the unknown density, she hears screaming echoed in the distance. Hugo is disciplining the woman who let her get away. He obviously is unaware the woman had failed to handcuff Jennifer again.

Not knowing which way to go and what lay ahead, Jennifer crouched down and tried to call 911 from the phone she grabbed. Her hands are shaking too severely, her heart pounding as if it would come out of her chest. She knew they would try to find her before she got too far. A man's voice shouted, "Come back, lady, we aren't going to hurt you. There are snakes and alligators out there. I have food for you." She is frightened out of her wits, but kept going looking for any sign of lights. It was very dark and starting to rain. She continually falls to the ground, sinking into the mud-soaked saw grass marshes. Her knees cut and bleeding from the saw grass, her ankle twisted. Saw grass is a member of the sedge family and is not really grass. It is named for the rows of sharp teeth that run along each edge and down the central spine. If touched in the wrong direction, it can be brutal. The area contains few trees and shrubs. Cattails prosper. She has become disoriented and light-headed from the remnants of the drugs.

Chapter Twenty-Seven

Desperate and exhausted, her fingers trembling, she is finally able to get 911. "Help me, please, my name is Jennifer and I have been kidnapped."

"Please stay on the line; where are you now?"

"I don't know, I just ran from a cabin, from a young woman and from a man named Hugo."

"Jennifer, what is your last name?"

"Aldrich, Jennifer Aldrich. I am in a swamp near a lake with a cabin. There may be a green van. I am afraid of snakes and alligators. Please help me."

"Jennifer, look around, do you see anything at all that you can identify?"

"I don't see any lights, no road. I see a fence. It is a chain-link fence. I am afraid they will come to look for me. They are still calling my name and I see a flash of light."

"Follow the fence. See if any markings are along the fence."

Jennifer, shaking, desperately followed the fence, continually falling into the wet swamp grass. "I see a sign on the fence; it's too dark to read." By the grace of God and a miracle, a cloud moved momentarily and she was able to read the sign. "It looks like 'Jasper Fence Company.'" A call was immediately relayed to the FBI and an emergency call was made to David Barr, who is in route to Miami. He immediately screeched the car to a halt, turned around, and started back toward Naples. Within minutes, a Black Hawk helicopter took off from the Homestead Air Force Base with FBI agents and a swat team aboard. The owner of the Jasper fence company stayed on the line to give directions to all the chained fences installed near swampy areas in the vicinity of Naples and Ft. Meyers. He remembered where a cabin might be.

"Jennifer, please stay on the line and tell me when you hear or see a helicopter or sirens. My name is Janice."

"The flashlight seems to be getting closer to me. Hugo is calling my name."

"Stay calm and just listen. If you have to talk, whisper. Just stay as low as you can. We have help on the way." Thirty minutes passed, but to Jennifer, whose face and body are almost devoured by the slime and mud, it seemed like hours. Her body is pressed flat into the ground, her clothes saturated with water, mud, and blood.

"Janice," Jennifer whispers, "I hear the helicopter in the distance. It is getting louder. Now I see the lights."

Ten minutes later, Janice says, "Jennifer, they have spotted a cabin with what appears to be a van parked outside. Jennifer, please keep your courage; it's almost over. You are going to be safe."

In a matter of minutes, the ground is swarming with patrol cars. Brilliant search lights are everywhere. The helicopter landed somewhere close by and Hugo Verga, a locally known hood, along with his battered girlfriend, Maria Perez, a nineteen-year-old high school drop-out, were taken into custody.

Several officers, with the precision you would expect in a combat zone, ran to the swamp away from the cabin, calling for Jennifer as the rain was coming down in torrents. Her voice is weak but she is able to call out until they are able to locate her. She is quickly put on a stretcher, covered with a blanket, and retrieved from the swamp. She is then airlifted to the Mayo Clinic in Naples, where she is found to be in good shape, except for a sprained ankle and multiple cuts and scratches. Luckily, she did not encounter any creatures she is so desperately afraid of.

CHAPTER TWENTY-EIGHT

Two hours later, David reached the hospital, where Jennifer cried in his arms for at least ten minutes. The people closest to the situation were informed of her safety, but word of her rescue could not be let out until after the time of the phone call that David is expecting, just in case it did still come through.

"Jen, I'm proud of you for the way you were able to get away. You even had the presence of mind to grab the phone. You are a brave young lady. If you hadn't grabbed the phone, you might have been in that swamp a lot longer."

"Oh! David, I was so frightened. I don't remember picking up the phone."

"Well, I need to keep a closer eye on you." She smiles and thanks him for coming to Florida to look for her. "By the way, there is another chap who has been worried about you. I have been camping at Dr. Bharne's home for the last two days."

"You have?"

"Yes, I called him right after you boarded the helicopter. He is pretty relieved. Jen, I have some business to take care of before I take you home. I want you to stay at the hospital until tomorrow, when I will be back for you." After making sure that she has ample protection, he kisses her tenderly on the forehead and starts back across Alligator Alley with Agent James to Miami and to Rab's house. Jennifer is given a mild sedative and antibiotics to ward off a threat of pneumonia, feeling secure and very close to David, who seems to have a special interest in her. "What does all this mean?" she says to herself, as she falls into a deep sleep. An FBI agent is positioned outside her private hospital room. No one goes in without his trained professional scrutiny.

Chapter Twenty-Nine

At Rab's house the next morning at 9:00 a.m. sharp, the phone rings. The necessary recording equipment operated by agents anxious to trace the call has been waiting.

David Barr responds to the caller who demands records that detail facial changes performed on two known crime figures in exchange for the safe return of Jennifer Aldrich. David keeps the caller talking as long as he can, pretending to be desperate for her safety. He pleads with the caller to give him more information about the documents in question, including specific times of the surgeries. He promises to do all he can to locate any data that would save Jennifer's life.

It is obvious, by the conversation, that the caller is somewhat of a novice at this type of crime. Ironically, he stays on the line long enough for the call to be traced to the Sea Urchin Motel near Ft. Lauderdale, Florida. In a matter of minutes after David hangs up, the Sea Urchin Motel is swarming with FBI and local police. One unshaven, disheveled, half-drunk individual registered as Jacob Malloy was arrested and promptly taken into custody. The name did not fit the description. Mr. Malloy was more Italian than Irish or Jewish.

David arrived to accompany Jennifer home the next morning. She looked a little tired, but dressed, ready for travel after having her luggage and purse retrieved from the cabin. Her cell phone is the only thing missing. The charter flight touched down in Macon a little before 2:00 p.m. A car was waiting to take them back to Middleton, where a lot of inquisitive and concerned friends and neighbors were waiting. Marsha Benning is given a more permanent task of watching over Jennifer. She is happy to do so, since she feels like one of the family, having also bonded with Fox. David arranged, through Mark Powers, for a temporary leave of absence to keep Jennifer out of public view. She made a brief call to Ms. Klara, assuring her she is all right and taking a vacation. The next morning, she, Marsha, and Fox are taken to an undisclosed location.

David called Rab to brief him on what is happening. He suggested to Rab it would be better, for his safety as well as Jen's, that they not contact one another during this crucial time. He understood.

Tuesday morning, David is able to reach the FBI lab and obtain the information about the DNA samples he had requested. The results are conclusive. He asked that the report not be given to anyone else without his okay.

Chapter Thirty

The weekend is approaching. Jennifer, Marsha, and Fox are becoming a great team. The North Carolina beach house where they are staying is surrounded by dunes, mounds or hills of sand created by dune grasses, which trap sand grains being moved across the beach by wind. Supplies are being brought in by a local FBI agent by the name of Art Cantrell, who is assigned along with Marsha to protect Jennifer.

Art is a thirty-five-year-old divorcee with two teenage boys that he has custody of. His lifestyle did not suit his former wife, who ran off with her hairdresser, a woman, to "seek her destiny."

The beach house is owned by a former classmate and acquaintance of David's, whom David had saved from self-destruction after graduating from Yale. His friend, Simon Cohen, after becoming a lawyer, became involved with a married woman who dumped him when she decided to remain with her husband. David moved in with Simon to protect him when he was thought to be suicidal. Simon got over his obsession, made lots of money, and is now happily married to the girl of his dreams. David, on the other hand, to date has no serious relationships with the opposite sex. He has opportunity and dates occasionally, but the dedication to his work is his obsession. He has found himself thinking about Jen, but always feels a reluctance to get closer.

The waters are calm, only an occasional sailboat or a freighter in the distance. Jennifer, looking more rested, and Marsha, never without her hidden weapon, cautiously look for unusual shells along the beach. Fox, running back and forth, has never had it so good. The wind is gentle and the air, clean. A slight chill warrants lightweight sweats and running shoes. This is not a bad predicament at present. Jennifer's mother had left her pretty well off financially, although she lives modestly. She has no money worries.

Chapter Thirty-One

David interrogated Mr. Malloy, or Guido Rosa, his real name. Guido is more than eager to sing like a bird to save his skin. He claims that he, Hugo (not knowing his last name), and Salvator Parini abducted the woman and her driver. The driver was shot by Salvator "because he could identify us." Hugo had a girlfriend who knew of a cabin where the girl was to be taken. The woman is to be kept alive until the boss in Chicago, Vinni Peche, received the information he wanted. Guido had been supplied with a script by an associate of Peche. "Where is Salvator Parini now?"

"He had been told by the boss to leave town and get back to Chicago after he killed the driver." Guido willingly gave the address.

"Where can we find Peche?"

"Nobody knows how to find him. He contacts us."

"How will he contact you and when do you expect to hear from him?"

"He will be calling my room. I don't know when." Having left someone in the room registered to "Malloy," the FBI found Salvator Parini's address through a phone call placed to Guido. It was the same as Guido had said. Parini was immediately located and arrested for murder. No calls came in from Peche or anyone else.

Rab promised Marcilene that Agent Barr would find her husband's killer and bring him to justice. The funeral for Raoul was attended by Rab as well as many of the population of the Hispanic community where the couple lived. "Marcilene is a strong woman and determined to get on with her life. She has quite a support system," Rab told David after being informed that the trigger man had been caught.

"Now, we have to find the mastermind behind all this."

"How is Jennifer?"

"She is getting along quite well and under a strong surveillance. I have not been in contact with her directly as yet. It is unclear what we are up against and I have been extremely busy. However, we are closer to solving a lot of the mystery. I will stay in touch."

"Thank you, David."

CHAPTER THIRTY-TWO

It was noon on Monday when David received the news. Trudy Panachek was actually Elizabeth Minotti. Her father, Giacomo Minotti, a notorious crime boss, along with his first lieutenant, Luigi Chiabrera, testified against leading Sicilian mafioso figures in Palermo ten years prior. They are both believed to be in the witness protection program.

Anthony Panachek, his actual name, according to sources, had been given a large sum of money by his girlfriend, known as Trudy, to start his own physical therapy business if he would relocate with her to Middleton, Georgia. The couple lived together for six years in Chicago in a remote cabin on Lake Michigan. It is thought that Elizabeth left the Windy City seeking to find the location of her father. Her mother died after passing on information she had been privy to about her father. For survival reasons, her parents were divorced. Her mother knew about the plastic surgery performed by a prominent doctor in Georgia, but not the details.

Her position at the telephone company enabled Elizabeth, known as Trudy Panachek, to obtain information leading her to Middleton, Georgia. The fact that she and Anthony moved into the neighborhood, becoming a neighbor of Jennifer Aldrich, was no accident. Tony Panachek was not as secretive as Elizabeth. They were easy targets for the killers, having been located through friends at his previous employment.

It becomes evident that Elizabeth and Tony were killed in an effort to flush her father out of hiding or to find his location. The puzzle is starting to come into place, although the suspects have not been publicly identified.

CHAPTER THIRTY-THREE

David, having suspected the true identity of Jen's father, must keep the information to himself for her protection, as well as safeguarding his investigation.

Vinni Peche sees himself as a powerful figure of a secret society called Camorra, originating in Sicily and organized in Naples, Italy, which became notorious for blackmail and terror. Peche avenges by means of terror and vendetta, and is heavily involved in drug trafficking, gambling, and loan sharking. He claims to have come from Palermo. The truth is, he was born in Chicago and had never been to Sicily. His great-grandparents emigrated from Palermo to Chicago during prohibition. His great-grandfather, Cesare Peche, was thought to have been involved in organized crime, but loyalty and intimidation of witnesses prevented charges to be brought against him or other known crime figures. Cesare Peche, Jr., Vinni's father, was sentenced for federal tax evasion and died in a federal prison in 1955 at the age of fifty-five. Vinni, always enamored by his grandfather's reputation, chose a life of crime.

As a teenager in Middleton, David remembered being approached by a man who looked to be about thirty years old. The man asked David if his parents were home; he claimed to want to speak to his dad about a medical matter. Although the investigating team had been aware of this after Dr. Barr's death, Detective Raymore could not find any substantial leads. David never forgot the man's appearance. He was heavy and dark-skinned, with a moustache. He spoke with what seemed to be an Italian accent. David has been conscientiously searching for this man for ten years. He knows now that finding him is inevitable.

CHAPTER THIRTY-FOUR

"Dr. Bharne is on the phone for you, Agent Barr." David answers as he thanks the secretary taking the call.

"Yes, Rab, how are you? What can I do for you?"

"I'm fine, thank you. I am planning to take a trip to Europe to escort my mother back home. I will be gone for about ten days. I wanted to touch base with you, to see if any new developments had occurred and to find out about Jennifer. Is she safe?"

"Yes! I feel confident she is safe. We are on the right track. I hope to have some information before too long. Have a nice trip, and please, feel free to call when you return. Hopefully, by then, I will have more to tell you."

"Thank you, I will contact you when I return."

"Take care!"

After a week of feeling pretty confident and safe at the beach house, Jennifer and Marsha are forming a sisterly relationship. Marsha told Jennifer about her broken marriage and Jennifer confided about past relationships, including the last, which was abusive. The two of them get along quite well, and have formed a friendship with Art Cantrell, the local agent sent as back-up protection. When bringing supplies, Art spends time with Fox, but Jennifer detects that Art is more interested in Marsha.

The three of them speak to passersby occasionally on the beach when jogging, but are careful not to have a conversation with anyone. Since Jennifer's picture was in all the papers before she was rescued, she wears sunglasses and always a hat when outside. It is fall now, but the weather is still pretty warm where they are. Jennifer is anxious to go home. She worries about Ms. Klara and not knowing what is happening. She also thinks about David. "What has he discovered? Poor Rab, he must be wondering what he got himself into. Will I ever see him again?"

With Salvator Parini and Guido Rosa both behind bars, Guido confesses that Parini, in addition to killing the chauffeur, is the one who killed the Panacheks. Guido claims that Vinni Peche found that Trudy Panachek is actually Elizabeth Minotti and gave the order to find them, stake out their home, and find out what they know about the location of Giacomo Minotti and Luigi Chiabrera. This, believed Peche, will give himself a big name with the Sicilian group and with the Salernos.

When the Panacheks arrived home after a three-day trip to the Keys, they surprised the intruders, and during the scuffle "Salvator panicked because of the commotion and killed them." Vinni Peche was unhappy about this, because they failed to get information, but he gave them a chance to redeem themselves by kidnapping one Jennifer Aldrich, whom he believed to be the illegitimate daughter of either Minotti or Chiabrera. Guido also claimed that people from Palermo ordered the killing of Dr. Barr, and killed Dr. Aldrich as well.

David, on the other hand, is not sure of this. There is a question as to whether Minotti and Chiabrera killed both doctors to keep them from identifying their new appearances. Concerning the claim that Jen is the daughter of Minotti or Chiabrera, David wants to know how they came to that conclusion.

According to sources, Dr. Janelle Aldrich became acquainted with

Minotti after the two met when she was a young medical student. She developed a friendship with him while attending a medical convention in Las Vegas. Becoming aware of some of his notorious activities, she was instrumental in persuading him to, in her words, "do the right thing." Soon after, Minotti contacted Dr. Aldrich, who set up an appointment for a consultation with Dr. Barr. Both Minotti and Chiabrera decided they were ready to change their lifestyles and go to the authorities for a plea bargain. Changing appearances was essential.

CHAPTER THIRTY-FIVE

Depositions at the time of Dr. Barr's untimely death indicated that Dr. Aldrich and also Dr. Barr were friendly with the two who had testified for the federal government against Sicilian mobsters operating in the United States. The two former gangsters were thought to have been put out of immediate danger by changing appearances and entering a witness protection program.

David falls asleep with a headache at his mother's home, thinking about all the obstacles and possibilities. Eva Barr is concerned about her son and about the profession to which he is so dedicated. The next morning, they enjoy breakfast together when she tries to engage David in small talk. "How is Jennifer? Has she recovered from her ordeal?"

"Yes, she has, Mother; hopefully, she will come to visit soon."

"I hope so, too. I really have gotten to like her."

" She will need some support, after she has time to rest." Eva does not ask where Jennifer is located.

"I am going to be at the downtown office, Mother. Please, call my cell phone if you need anything. I have asked Hans not to leave you alone."

"Don't worry about us, son. This place is a fortress. I feel very safe. You take care of yourself."

Reports of increased drug trafficking, prostitution, and loan sharking that have infiltrated into some smaller areas outside of major cities including Chicago and Las Vegas are of immediate concern to the authorities. The FBI has information leading to a group of crime figures headed by one Vinni Peche. His location is as secret as Bin Laden's whereabouts. The group is being watched by undercover agents who plan to gain sufficient evidence for prosecution and Peche's whereabouts before apprehension. This is somewhat of a Hollywood wise-guy operation.

At the office, David holds an intelligence briefing with several agents to know the enemy. Peche is the number-one target and priority at present. Authorities know he has two older sisters living in the Cincinnati area who do not want to have any contact with him and have not seen or heard from him since their mother died in 2001. Peche is not married, but known to have two regular girlfriends. One, an exotic dancer at a well-known strip club called Members, Etc. and frequented by mobsters, is in Chicago. The other, a bartender working at a posh hotel, is located in Miami in the Coconut Grove area. Both women are being watched around the clock. Their phones are constantly monitored by the agency.

David deems it necessary to proceed through channels to locate Minotti and Chiabrera. This effort could be of big help to finding Peche if all else fails. He also has a personal reason for locating the two for whom his father performed identity change surgery. Do they have information on his father's murder?

It is 11:30 p.m. on Friday when a dancer, Angelina Ros, billed as Angel in Members, Etc., strikes up a conversation with a patron who noticeably is becoming a regular customer.

Jake Jaffey is a former counterintelligence agent who switched to criminal cases. It is common knowledge that counterintelligence agents and criminal agents view one another as being dumb or lazy, but the FBI is a diversified agency effectively working former foreign counterintelligence agents into other programs. Jaffey, during the Cold War, was a major player in some of the world's most important sensitive espionage cases of all time. His training has taught him to be successful at meeting and talking to people on different levels. His appointed mission at present is to become acquainted with one Angelina Ros and dissect information about her associates, including Vinni Peche. His patience and aloofness has prompted Angel to approach him.

CHAPTER THIRTY-SIX

"Hi! My name is Angel. Do you mind if I sit down?" He nods nonchalantly and she joins him at his table. After a brief conversation about weather and the club amenities, he confides that he is a recent widower and proceeds to gain her trust by giving some details of a bogus life.

"Will you be in tomorrow?"

"If I can, I will try." It didn't take many nights after his initial meeting with her to appear as a loyal fan, gain her confidence, and start driving her home after work. Although she is inquisitive about his work and where he lives, he is known only to her as Patrick Nichols, "sort of an entrepreneur" living downtown. She decides he is a very private person and does not pursue further questioning. Angelina, on the other hand, seems to live beyond her means in a penthouse overlooking Lake Erie. Jake uses every opportunity he can to get into her apartment. He is able to take pictures of photographs placed around her rooms when she is busy fixing drinks or changing. Finally, after delicately probing, he gets her to tell him about her lover, Vinni. "Do you see him often? Does he live in Chicago?"

"No, he lives in Vegas, but comes in quite often."

"Do you expect him anytime soon? I would not want to be here when he arrives. He may get the wrong idea."

"He usually gives me a few hours' notice. He is a salesman and travels a lot." Jake is aware that Angel knows more about Vinni than she is willing to divulge. Her apartment building will now be placed on priority alert.

Back at the FBI criminal lab, some of the pictures Jake was able to obtain and develop were obviously of Vinni Peche. A vivid description is important, but what is more important is the background. In two of the photographs, the background revealed details of a particular boat dock, and another, a French restaurant located at the MGM in Vegas. This could be a major break.

Jennifer is starting to get restless. She has tired of the beach. Some days are gloomy, now that fall is approaching. The rain is more prevalent and her reading material is starting to disinterest her. The only people with whom she has contact are her protectors. It is obvious that although discreet, Marsha and Agent Cantrell are becoming closer. This is a good thing, but Jennifer can't help feeling isolated and lonely. Fox is a pleasure and gives her reason to exercise, running alongside him.

David called about 9:30 p.m. on the cell phone he had given her. "Jen, how are you?"

"David, I am so happy to hear from you. When will I be able to return home?"

"We have made some progress and I believe it will be soon. I am planning to stop to see you on my way to another location. I will tell you about it when I arrive tomorrow. Art is convinced you need a little TLC."

"So, Art has picked up on my mood. Very observant!"

Jennifer finds herself overjoyed, looking forward to David's visit. "Will he provide any answers?"

Chapter Thirty-Seven

Jennifer and Marsha are accustomed to rising early. They are prepared when David arrives at 11:00 a.m. He is accompanied by agents, Tilford and Hayes. It is a welcome change for Jennifer, and also for Marsha, to have some company. They are delighted to see familiar faces. Agent Art Cantrell arrives at 11:30 a.m. to be included in an extensive briefing of the events and strategy to be taken.

Jennifer busies herself preparing lunch and is included but not privy to planned details of sophisticated techniques used by the agents to approach intended targets. She is impressed by what she hears and again feels the security of having David take care of her. "Jen, I want you to know that Rab is in touch with me. He is concerned about your safety. I told him I would keep him up-to-date, but that it was not a good idea for him to be in touch with you directly until we make some major breaks. He is traveling abroad at this time and plans to escort his mother home from London."

"Thank you. I was wondering what he thought of all this. I really enjoyed my time with him."

The trio left before nightfall to board a small private plane headed for Vegas. At the Vegas airport they were met by Agent Jake Jaffey, who presented recent black and white photographs of Vinni Peche. Equipped with the knowledge obtained by Jaffey from Angel, along with the photographs he was able to take and several photos of known associates of Peche, their confidence of breaking this case is increasing. The ATF had given the bureau a list of dealers known to be in the region. The goal is to infiltrate a local drug cartel and hopefully bring national crime figures to justice. In addition, David is eager to capture Vinni Peche. After checking in at the MGM, the four agents scouted around the crowded casinos, looking for familiar faces. It was a long day and night. Jaffey, who is the least known face because of his recent transfer to criminal, has the task of locating and befriending contacts within the drug cartel. His special organizational skills are of great importance.

The next morning proved to be more promising. Jake Jaffey made contact with his informant in a local garage who gave specific locations known to be frequented by local drug users. The four agents again split up and worked shifts from 7:00 a.m. until 11:00 p.m. and 11:00 p.m. until 7:00 a.m. for three days. Jake, positioning himself on a stool at the bar in a small lounge located three blocks from the MGM, became acquainted with Silly Silky Sylvester, a fast-talking, slight-in-stature, balding individual with penetrating gray eyes. Jake's experience, knowledge, and patience from having been in counterintelligence soon led to bragging to Silky, as he prefers to be called. Upon gaining an obvious flicker of trust from this eager-to-be-important little man drenched in gold chains, Jake claims to be looking for friends who promised to put him in touch with sellers having Sicilian contacts.

CHAPTER THIRTY-EIGHT

After a little small talk and several pauses, Silky speaks. "I can be of help to you, but I'm not able to give you information now. If you meet me tomorrow at Charlie's Diner across town at 4:00 p.m., I will have someone you can talk to." Silky has always been credited with having the brain of a moron. His association with crime figures has given him a self-inflicted sense of importance. The people he is attached to use him as a gopher and, if need be, he is expendable and could be used as a scapegoat.

"This someone, is he involved with La Cosa Nostra?" La Cosa Nostra is an Italian phrase meaning "this thing is ours," and is often referred to as the Mafia or mob.

"I can't say. If you have the money, I have contacts."

"Okay, I will see you tomorrow."

Agents Barr, Hayes, and Tilford meet with Agent Jaffey later in the hotel room and go over what each has learned. David, intent on finding Peche, had mentioned his name to a couple informants who claimed not to know how to locate him. However, the photograph shown to one hotel manager sparked a visible interest. The man in the photo, known as Joe Salerno, according to the reservations clerk, has been registered at the MGM for two weeks. This is the break worth waiting for. Immediately, Operation Wild Game was put into effect. The FBI creates code names for major cases. This is a lot quicker and more efficient to identify a case.

Before moving in on the targeted suspects, it is important to gather intelligence on their activities. The FBI is notified and a surveillance team of several agents is summoned for a stake-out. Suite 2923, occupied by the person believed to be Vinni Peche, is vacant at the moment. The adjoining room is promptly taken over by the three FBI agents and equipped with eavesdropping devices, audio and visual.

At 3:00 p.m. the next day, Agent Jake Jaffey, watching Charlie's Diner through binoculars from his blue Cadillac from a half-block distance, sees a man and woman looking to be in their forties enter the diner at exactly 3:37 p.m. The two sit at the end of a booth, one facing the entrance, the other facing the window. At ten minutes before four, Silky arrives. He nonchalantly nods to the couple and places himself near the door. He sits alone.

Exactly at 3:59, Jake, dressed casually but prosperously, entered the restaurant. He is greeted by Silky. "Hello! I'm sorry, I do not remember your name."

" I prefer to remain anonymous at this time. You understand? There is a lot at stake here; I am sticking my neck out, and if you can't help me, I will be on my way." With this said, Silky squirms a little and makes a commitment to introduce Jake to someone of importance that can possibly supply what he is in the market to buy. Silky can't help but think of his cut and the respect he will gain. The couple in the restaurant, having heard the conversation, immediately show an interest in Jake and approach the two men. They introduce themselves as Joe Salerno and Ms. Martin. Jake realizes he is face-to-face with Vinni Peche and a notorious female assassin known by the FBI as Rhonda Borg.

With an obvious nod by Joe Salerno, Silky excuses himself and nervously exits the restaurant, leaving the trio to conduct business. Any attempt for Jake to contact his fellow agents at this point would be too risky. He agrees to accompany the couple to another location where, in their words, he would be able to sample the merchandise.

Chapter Thirty-Nine

Upon arriving at an out-of-the-way, run-down building near an abandoned railroad, secluded by brush and rusty rail cars, Jake is scrutinized by the couple. He shows them his bogus identification, which, after careful examination, the two seem to be satisfied by, but they continue to keep a careful watch. Jake, in return, pretends to examine the validity of their claims to be able to supply the equipment and drugs he is interested in buying. All the while they are attempting to convince him, he is making a close superficial survey and critical observation of the minutest details of their location and the conversation taking place. This is not the time for critical errors.

The next meeting to exchange monies for an enormous amount of drugs being flown in from South America, they claim, and also a truckload of assault weapons, which are housed in a Vegas warehouse, will take place in two days.

Jake did not give the name of his hotel and kept a watchful eye on anyone who may be trailing him. He carefully made several stops at various clubs and did not use a telephone where he can be observed.

Finally, when he is able to contact David and the other agents, Operation Wild Game took another turn and the agents prepared to wait for the exchange.

Suite 2923 is still under heavy surveillance with the FBI and ATF teams next door.

In the early days, Hoover had refused to let the FBI become involved in drug investigations. This was changed in 1989 when violent crimes, worked by the FBI, were elevated to a higher priority. Drug crimes are related to murder-by-hire, bank robberies, high jacking and assaults on officers.

Now that he was seen by Peche and the woman, Jake will have to stay away from the hotel. Two ATF agents dressed as homeless derelicts are quickly sent to the railroad warehouse where Jake's meeting had taken place. Everything necessary is put into motion to gather evidence and make arrests. All they have to do now is wait and observe.

Back at the beach house, Jennifer is getting anxious to get back to what used to be a normal life for her. She thinks about the few wonderful days with Rab and prays for the safety of David and his team. Marsha continues to be upbeat, ensuring that everything will work out and permit them to leave soon for home.

CHAPTER FORTY

It is about 2:00 on Saturday afternoon when Rab and his mother deplaned at the Miami airport, returning from Europe. The trip was exhausting for his mother, who always seems to be in good health otherwise. The two returned home to find that Marcilene, in spite of grieving over the sudden murder of her husband, had the house in order and a delightful snack prepared.

Rab is not due back at the Mount Sinai hospital until Monday. However, on Sunday, his surgical nurse, Jillian, called and asked that he meet her at the hospital to go over the surgery schedule for the next day, which he agreed to do. She appeared worried about a potentially critical heart patient of another doctor who is scheduled for back surgery and wanted his input. The two exchanged pleasantries; she appeared to be genuinely interested in his trip and the places he visited. "Jillian, I think you are right to be concerned about this patient, but Dr. Allen, who has asked me to scrub, has taken every precaution not to put this patient at unnecessary risk. The patient himself understands the procedure and has opted to proceed. I agree with the patient that he has a better chance at a normal life than if we did nothing."

"By the way," she says, turning to Rab as he is about to leave. "I have two tickets to the opera on Wednesday and thought you might need a break. It is *Salome*. The fact is, I need an escort."

"Thank you, Jillian. That sounds very nice. I do enjoy the opera and have no plans; I would be most happy to be your escort." Treating the invitation as he would one by any fellow worker with whom he has mutual respect, he asks if he should pick her up or meet at the hospital.

"No, this is my treat. I would like to pick you up, say about 7:00 p.m.?"

"Well now, that sounds like a plan. I will map out directions to my home and bring them tomorrow."

"Thanks again. I will look forward to Wednesday." Jillian cannot contain her glee when she walks away, pretending not to know where he lives. She has finally gotten Dr. Abraham Bharne to go on a date. Having seen the interest he portrayed in Jennifer Aldrich gave her a little more urgent incentive to act upon her long-term desires to get him alone and have his undivided attention. This is her big chance and she will be careful not to blow it.

CHAPTER FORTY-ONE

Seven hours have passed since Jake's meeting with Vinni Peche, alias Joe Salerno, and the hit woman. They have not been seen near Salerno's suite. FBI agents still wandering around the casinos are hoping to pick up a trail to follow when Vinni appears at the door to his suite. The key is inserted and the door opens. He goes directly to the desk telephone and has a brief conversation with the front desk. "I am expecting three gentlemen at 11:00 p.m. Please have them call before they come up." The conversation is important to the surveillance team. They notify Jake, who promptly places a team in the lobby near the front desk, hoping to identify any or all of three men asking for Mr. Salerno. Rhonda Borg, alias Ms. Martin, is nowhere in sight.

It is September, and the temperature is 109 degrees and stifling hot as the two-man team waits in place at the railroad yard near the warehouse where the weapons are thought to be stored. The area is remote, surrounded by mounds of brush and high weeds, and cluttered with trash left by the local hobos. A skinny dog ravages through the debris and finds nothing edible before wandering off. No self-respecting canine would spend much time here. The hungry homeless barely leave enough trash for one another.

After trying to nose around the warehouse, the two agents are chased off by a security guard and decide to observe from a distance, from inside an old abandoned rail car.

At ten minutes before 11:00, a man approached the hotel desk and asked for Mr. Salerno's room number. After he is told to contact the room by phone, he nodded and is joined by two men who had been in the lobby for forty-five minutes reading newspapers and obviously observing. Not having detected the surveillance team, they seemed to be satisfied that it is safe to go to the elevator leading to Suite 2923.

The agents in Suite 2925 are notified and ready to watch and listen when the men entered next door and are greeted by Vinni Peche. They called him Joe. An ATF agent positioned in the room along with the FBI recognized one of the men to be Myron Garcia, a once well-known and gifted football player sought after by the big leagues, but who decided he could make more money in dealing. He has been under investigation for drug trafficking for fourteen months. The conversation started out casually until Vinni proceeded to tell about the big fish he had on the hook willing to give big bucks for weapons and drugs. Specifically ordered were nine-millimeter semiautomatic pistols, Ruger-14, and Colt AR-15 assault rifles. They discussed not being able to come up with the Ruger-14 semiautomatic carbine rifles, which can penetrate car doors, not to mention bullet-proof vests. Drugs are open to just about anything from crack to cocaine and heroin. In other words, Jake claimed to be in the market for anything marketable and available at a reasonable price. It is not yet mentioned where the drugs or weapons are located.

Back at the railroad warehouse, the two undercover ATF agents posing as homeless observed two large gray trucks backing into the warehouse. This is immediately relayed to the other teams, who watched for signs of activity. All they have to do now is continue to wait, eat fast food, and drink plenty of coffee. The action is expected to take place the next day at noon, when Jake has promised to bring the cash to the warehouse. It promises to be a long night. The teams are in place, concealed outside the area surrounding the warehouse and the railroad yard. They doze in shifts. The hotel room is quiet where Vinni and his friends are located, until Madam Rhonda Borg arrives with two women, obviously hookers. The group partied into early morning, after which the women were told the party is over. They gathered their belongings and money on the way out the door and promptly vanished. Rhonda stayed behind to glorify in the planned activity of the day. The prostitutes seemed to be of no significance, and therefore not followed.

CHAPTER FORTY-TWO

High noon couldn't come soon enough for the agents. The criminals are anxious as well, thinking they will be paid a healthy sum of money. It is 11:00 a.m. when a late-model black Pontiac sedan, a rental, first drove to the warehouse followed by an older-model Ford SUV. The sedan contained Vinni Peche, and two unidentified men. Myron Garcia drove the SUV with two passengers armed with sub-machine guns. The group entered the warehouse with the exception of the two with machine guns. They are greeted by two security guards and the two truck drivers. It is believed that two men are on lookout while a group of nine remains inside. All are expected to be armed.

The stage is set. The buyer must appear to be genuine; there is too much at stake. Jake Jaffey arrives exactly at noon, being driven by an ATF agent that he will describe as his counterpart, whom he brought as a security. The agent will stay cautiously at a distance inside the car. Jake emerges from the blue Cadillac carrying two large attaché cases containing money. The stacks of bills are genuine on the tops and on the bottoms of each, but the middle of each stack is filled with blank papers.

Jake is greeted by Vinni who promptly asks to see the money. The attaché cases are opened briefly by Jake and then closed. "Lets see what you have before we go any further."

The truck containing firearms is intensely inspected by Jake, who then asked about the other purchase, meaning drugs. "You will be pleased. We were able to come up with several cases of ecstasy pills in addition to your request."

'It looks like things are in order here. I will just signal my man outside that everything is okay and he can make arrangements to empty the trucks." Jake goes to the door as he is closely observed by the group inside. He gives a thumbs up, and without advance warning, the building and the perimeter is dominated by FBI, ATF, and local police. The two armed gunmen keeping watch had been apprehended without incident. This seemed like one smooth operation. However, Vinni Peche was not going to give up that easily, nor was hit woman, Rhonda Borg. With exceptional speed, Vinni's loose coat opened, from which he grabbed a Cadix 38 Snub nose out of a leather holster and began firing. He ducked into one of the trucks and was able to wound two of the agents before he was dragged out and put into handcuffs. Rhonda, on the other hand, eluded the officers and attempted to escape through a back door. She fired two shots from her revolver and fatally wounded a local police officer before David was able to slam her to the ground, breaking her nose. "This is one hit woman that will be taken out of commission for good." The area is swarmed with ambulances and police cars. The injured are taken to the hospital along with the slain police officer, a veteran of twenty-four years with the force, a big loss to his family and to the local police department. "Rhonda will indeed pay for this one," David comments sadly.

Vinni Peche is interrogated immediately upon being taken into custody. He refuses to talk about any connection to the Panachek murders or the murder of Dr. Barr. However, the evidence against him is sufficient to go to trial for murder, drug trafficking, harboring a dangerous female hit woman, prostitution, and the list goes on. Myron Garcia, along with the others, will also go to trial. This is a big bust, which will lead to other arrests. The only regret is the slain policeman.

CHAPTER FORTY-THREE

It is 4:00 p.m. when David telephones Marsha. "It's over; tell Jen to get packed. I am coming to take her home." Overjoyed at the news, Jennifer starts to cry. Marsha, on the other hand, has mixed emotions. She and Art Cantrell have developed a relationship which they plan to pursue.

"Jennifer, I have some time off and will stay around for a couple of days with Art. I know everything will be good with you and David. It's obvious he cares a great deal about you and will see that you are safe. I will stay in touch and see you as soon as I get back."

"Marsha, I can't thank you enough for your support and your patience. You are a good friend and I will miss you." Jennifer is ready and waiting when David arrives to escort her back home by a private jet that night. Hays and Tilford stay behind to wrap up the paperwork and continue processing all those in custody. The interrogation has only begun.

"It is so wonderful to wake up in my own bed," she says to herself the next morning. Fox is equally happy to be in familiar surroundings as he sniffs from room to room.

She immediately makes plans to return to work within a few days before she visits Ms. Klara, who is eager to see her. "Ms. Klara, you have a special glow about you; what have you been up to?"

"Nothing, dear, I am so happy you are home. It is lonely here without you." The two sit down for tea, when Jennifer notices Klara has a *Miami Herald*, which she begins to glance through. On the society page, she is startled to see a familiar face.

The caption reads, "Dr. Abraham Bharne, a renowned surgeon at Mt. Sinai Hospital and his date, Miss Jillian Kendall, are among several celebrities attending *Salome* at the opera." This is a little disturbing to her, but she has no recognizable reason to claim his undivided attention. After all, why should she care if he dates other women? This does prevent her from calling him as she intended to do as soon as possible.

"I will just write a note to him thanking him for the wonderful weekend and telling him that I am home safe."

"What did you say, dear?"

"I'm sorry, Ms. Klara, I was thinking out loud."

Chapter Forty-Four

The next few days are busy, catching up, cleaning her condo, running errands, and preparing to go back to work. She did manage to call David's mother to check on her and tell her what a wonderful son she has. Eva Barr expressed her relief to hear from her and to know that she and David are both safe. The two made plans for lunch the next week on her day off.

The work week started out pretty routinely on Monday. She was greeted by several fellow employees who expressed how happy they are to see her back. A few asked how her vacation went. It was Wednesday when Marsha called to chat. She is so happy to have time to spend with Art and his sons. Thursday is Jennifer's day off and lunch with Mrs. Barr. The two enjoyed each other's company immensely. The conversation centered on David, of course. Mrs. Barr confided that David always felt regret that he had not been able to prevent his father's murder. "There was nothing he could do. He might have been harmed himself had he been at home. I worry about David's job, but he is so happy doing what he does, and I understand he is quite good at it."

"I can certainly vouch for that. I am fortunate to have the two of you in my life."

"We feel the same about you, dear. Since you have been in our lives, I feel I have become closer to David." Just as they are about to leave the

98

restaurant, Jennifer looks across the room and notices Ms. Klara having lunch with Dr. Kleinman. She smiles to herself.

"So, this is why she is so glowing. Good for her, and him."

It has been several days since she has heard from David when he calls to tell her that Rab has been in touch with him. "He expected to hear from you."

"I know, David. I have reason to believe he is in a relationship and didn't want to interfere. I plan to send him a note. I just haven't gotten around to doing that yet."

"Okay, but he is anxious to hear from you."

"Thanks, David, I will get in touch with him."

"By the way, we need to get together. I have some things I want to discuss with you. When will you be free?"

"I'm off on Saturday."

"What about lunch on Saturday? I'll pick you up at 11:30 and we can drive to Macon."

"That's good, see you then."

Friday after work, Jennifer attempts to write a note to Rab.

Dear Rab,

Please accept my apologies to you for not writing sooner. When I was away, I could not let anyone know my where-abouts. When I returned, I found myself overwhelmed with chores and catching up.

I want to thank you for such a lovely time in Florida. I appreciate your gift of friendship and wish you the best for the future. Thanks to David, I have been well protected and feeling much safer.

Sincerely,

Jennifer Aldrich

Saturday, David drove up exactly at 11:30 a.m. to pick her up. The two shared conversation about the past events and how everything was progressing. "Are you closer to finding your father's killer?"

"We're on the right track, although I'm pretty sure it wasn't Vinni; he had a desire to make a name for himself, but I fail to see a motive. I believe Dad was killed for not giving up the identity of surgeries he performed on notorious crime figures. I also have reason to believe your mother was assassinated for the same reason. She was privy to information and assisted the same patients."

"Then you don't think my mother was killed accidentally?"

"No, I do not. I'm sorry to have to tell you this. If I wasn't quite sure, I would not tell you." Jennifer takes a moment to regain her composure.

"Will it ever be solved?"

"You can count on it." They pull up to a small restaurant outside Macon and sit down to lunch.

Chapter Forty-Five

"Jennifer"—she knows when he calls her Jennifer, it is serious—"I have another reason for wanting to be alone with you today. I have news about your father."

"OH?"

"Winston Gates, listed on your birth certificate, according to our sources, was a close friend of your mother and prompted her to put his name on the birth certificate to protect her and you. There is a strong possibility he is not your biological father. He has a brother, a retired physician living in Europe. I have made plans to visit him next week. I thought you might like to come along. We might clear up some of the mystery."

"Yes, I would like that very much."

"Good, I will make the arrangements. Now let's enjoy our lunch. Have you heard from Miami?"

"No, I sent a letter to Rab, but I haven't heard from him. I believe him to have a love interest at the hospital. I saw his picture recently in the society page of the *Miami Herald* attending the theatre with a nurse. I met this particular nurse and it was obvious to me she is definitely interested in him."

"I am sorry. He seemed genuinely interested in developing a relationship with you."

Preparation for the trip to Europe is exciting to Jennifer. She is looking forward to the trip, but most of all, to the possibilities of answers to so many questions about her mother and her own biological background. As she always does prior to leaving for a few days, Jennifer visits with Ms. Klara. The two enjoy a cup of tea and talk about the mysteries concerning the Panachek murders. Jennifer quickly changed the conversation to more pleasantries and her trip, a mini-vacation to Europe.

Ms. Klara is in exceptionally good spirits and seemingly better health. One can only wonder if this can be attributed to her relationship with Dr. Kleinman. When suggested, Ms Klara only blushes. "Please, come back safe from your trip and have a wonderful time." They embrace and say their goodbyes.

Chapter Forty-Six

When Rab received the note from Jennifer, he is surprised at the formality. He came to the conclusion that she is becoming closer to David. He disappointedly decided not to respond to her letter. The next few days are difficult for him to keep his concentration. He realized his feelings for Jennifer were stronger than he was aware of. His mother, concerned about his mood, asked if he was all right and if there was anything he wanted to discuss. "Mother, I thought I finally found the right woman to possibly want for your daughter-in-law, but it didn't work out. I'll be fine. I guess I'm just not used to rejection. Now, you get dolled up; I am taking you to the best restaurant in town and you are going to cheer me up."

The flight from Atlanta to London was the first overseas flight for Jennifer, who had not traveled extensively. She is excited about the enormity of the plane and all the perks. The two of them relaxed in the Business Elite section of a Delta B-777. The plane accommodated 277 passengers, 52 Business Elite and 225 Economy. There are only seven planes of this kind in service. Each one of the persons in Business Elite rows one through thirteen are given a small satiny cosmetic bag containing a tooth brush, tooth paste, ear plugs, a "Do Not Disturb" sign, a plastic box of Q-tips, a packet of Kleenex, mouth wash, lip balm, Tylenol, and skin moisturizer. In the seat pocket, besides magazines and duty-free Information, are individual cellophane packages containing earphones, an eye mask, and pair of black socks. A blanket is placed in every seat. The seats are oversized and can be extended flat for sleeping.

After being airborne, the hustle and bustle of the flight attendants became evident as they prepared carts of drinks and trays of food in a meticulously organized manner.

After four hours of flight time, Jennifer began to relax and put her thoughts of Winston Gates, her mother, and all that had happened to rest. She looked over at David, who had fallen asleep, and realized how important this man is to her and how safe she feels in his presence.

In the morning, daylight is coming through the windows and again the flight crew prepared another meal as the fifty-two passengers in the forward cabin scrambled to use one of the two lavatories in that section. The gentleman across the aisle, with whom she had spoken briefly, and whose name she couldn't pronounce, disappeared for quite some time with his carry-on flight bag. When he returned to his seat, he smelled of cologne and looked refreshed, as if he had taken time to shave, etc. The passengers are given a card to fill out for customs and an offer of a hotel voucher for a shower. Jennifer barely had time to visit the lavatory, comb her hair, put on lipstick, and pop gum into her mouth before replacing the complimentary socks with her shoes. They deplaned down a steep metal stair at Gatwick Airport in London to several waiting buses to take all 277 passengers of Delta Flight 12 to the air terminal where they would then line up in several lines to go through customs. The bus they are on has no seats left, leaving them to drag themselves and a carry-on.

After one and one-half hours, a bus hired by the hotel lines dropped them off at Grafton Hall Hotel on Tottenham Court Road. The two adjoining rooms are handsomely decorated. Jennifer's room is equipped with twin beds, bordered by bedside tables, each with a telephone. Two soft chairs and a small table placed in front of connecting windows decorated with plain sheers and draw drapes with red, blue, green, and yellow flowers on an off-white background provides a feeling of luxury. The drapes, displaying a two-foot valance, are held back by matching braided fabric. The padded headboards are covered with the same drapery fabric. The carpet is a medium red, with circled designs of wheat linking to small green patterns. The walls are covered with pale pink and white vertical striped wallpaper. There are pastel prints in gold frames of young ladies and pretty flowers placed on the walls. The room is elegant and relaxing.

Outside, overlooking a four-foot white railing in front of the windows, Jennifer can see a main street with restaurants and outside café tables. "What a lovely place to be."

After a two-hour nap, a gentle knock at the door by David inviting her to go for a late lunch prompted her to return to reality and the reason they are in London. She quickly showered and dressed for walking before meeting David in the hotel lounge.

After a casual meal at one of the outside cafés, David produced a *London Keys Guide*, a map provided by the hotel concierge. He pointed out some places of interest they may have time to visit before they return home. He then pointed out the area where Dr. Canfield Gates is known to reside. "I will contact Mr. Gates and try to schedule a meeting for tomorrow."

"That sounds good, David. I hope we can get some answers."

"Tonight, I want us to have a leisurely evening and get plenty of rest. We may have a big day tomorrow. Right now, I want to take you to the River Thames for a ride on the *Eye of London*. We can see a long way on as clear a day as today and I think you will enjoy a little diversion."

"Thank you, David, you are so thoughtful; I am fortunate to have you in my life."

The next morning, they met at breakfast at 8:00 a.m. in the hotel dining room. David had talked to Mr. Gates's nephew, William Gates, and arranged to have a meeting at 2:00 p.m. "David, I am excited but apprehensive about what I will learn."

"I know." He softly holds her hands in his.

CHAPTER FORTY-SEVEN

The Chicago headlines read, "NOTED CRIME FIGURE, VINNI PECHE ESCAPES FROM CUSTODY DURING INITIAL PROCEEDINGS PRIOR TO MURDER TRIAL. TWO ARE INJURED." Marsha immediately gets in touch with Art, who has been briefed by the FBI office in Chicago.

"Marsha, this is a critical situation. Vinni has vowed to finish his mission to find and eliminate Minotti and Chiabrera, both of whom are known to be inside the witness protection program. The Chicago office has found out that besides wanting to make a name for himself in the crime world, Vinni has a bigger vendetta against Luigi Chiabrera, who was suspected of slaying a step-brother of Peche." The step-brother, Andy Peche, a drug smuggler addicted to heroin, was not known to be violent. "We believe that Peche's escape was orchestrated by two of his henchmen, known only as Hicks and Claudy. It was a carefully planned scheme to grab Peche at the most vulnerable moment in the hall of the Justice Department as he was being led to the courtroom."

"How did they get past security into the hall?"

"They were dressed in clothes worn by guards, stolen from a uniform store. They were equipped with the same firearms the police carry. One guard and an attorney were injured; the guard's condition is serious, but not life-threatening. The attorney was shot in the leg."

"What is next?"

"We have all been put back on the case. I am to meet with Tilford and Hays at the Chicago office tomorrow. David is being notified as we speak, and you will be expected to stay close to Jennifer when they return from London. Nobody will be safe until this man is caught. He thinks of himself as a martyr."

"Please, be careful, Art."

"I will and you as well. I will stay in touch."

Vinni, Claudy, and Hicks are well on their way to hideout in a small fishing camp secluded by the marshes at the Isle of Capri in southern Florida.

It is an unusually beautiful sunny September day in the eighties as David and Jen board a two-decker bus on the way to Regent's Park to view the Queen's garden. They witnessed the aftermath of two separate weddings before resting on a bench with lunch consisting of hot dogs and lemonade. They walked along pathways lined with assortments of beautiful flowers, and to St. John's Harbor to the Secret Garden, a large garden room known by few tourists. A bench centered in the Secret Garden is arched by green foliage. Statues, carved in stone, modeled in a plastic substance or cast in bronze are throughout all the gardens; some personify beautiful people and others are in animal form. The calm, warm air after a morning rain is infused with the scent of roses that artfully grace the walkways.

"Tomorrow, we will go to the Wallace Collection Museum, where there are magnificent paintings from artists from all over the world. Any one painting would be a focal point in a United States museum."

"David, this is a wonderful experience. I almost forgot why we are here."

"I am so happy to bring you to this place for the first time; it is a special place to me. Now it is time to catch a cab and keep our appointment with Mr. Gates."

Chapter Forty-Eight

His cell phone rings, and after a brief conversation, changes his expression to alarming concern. "David, what is wrong?"

"It seems that our notorious Mr. Peche has escaped with a little outside help." Jen responds with a look of anguish and a frightened deep sigh. "Don't worry, he will leave a trail. Hayes and Tilford are back on the case, along with Marsha, who is looking after your place. We will talk about the possibilities later when I am able to get more information."

The cab pulled onto an elegant street of well-proportioned Palladian-style townhouses. Number 127 was in the middle of the block. The light gray, two-story building has black shutters that are meticulously clean. The steps leading down to the front door displayed a beautifully polished lion door knocker. Two window boxes, one on each side of the door, are neatly planted with an array of red flowers. They are greeted by William, the nephew of Canfield Gates, and led into the library of what appeared to be a *garconniere* or bachelor's quarters. Jennifer wondered if William is an heir presumptive or if Mr. Gates has other family members. He seems to be affluent by the manner in which he lives.

It is 6:30 a.m. on Monday morning in Miami as Rab prepares to scrub for surgery. Although his was a brief courtship of Jennifer Aldrich, he unwittingly finds himself profiling the silhouette of her face in his mind more frequently. "Could this be an illusion of what might have been?" He has always calculated and defined his future with determination and set out to investigate his every direction. It wasn't until he became aware of the grave danger Jennifer faced when he realized his feelings for her are more than dispassionate. Attempts to desensitize and dispel images of her are requiring extra effort. The frequent dates with Jillian are without warmth of feeling and nothing more than social engagements to Rab. Her continued expressions of possession and control characterized by her desires cause him to reach a decision to discontinue a personal relationship with her. Influences of her response to his rejection created by external personal circumstances are now threatening the workplace. Rab is compelled to ask for her transfer to another section in the hospital, where she will "be a more productive asset to other doctors." He vows emphatically to make a resolution to not fraternize with fellow employees, except during a casual atmosphere governed by chance.

Upon returning home after a full day in the OR, Rab and his mother have a casual dinner and relax on his boat docked behind their home. The air is fresh and calm, cooler than usual. Rab is comfortable talking to her about the circumstances leading up to asking that the nurse with whom he has been spending time be transferred out of his section of the hospital. She is not surprised; she met Jillian briefly but made her own decision, thinking, "This woman is more interested in my son than he is in her."

"I'm sorry, dear; I do, however, know you will find the right woman when the time is right and when you least expect to." He doesn't mention Jennifer, but she is in his thoughts. He wonders about her relationship with David and if she is happy.

"I should call David to see if any progress has been made."

"What did you say, dear?"

"Oh! I was just thinking out loud. I should call David Barr and get an update on his investigation."

"Hm!" Mrs. Bharne suspects she knows what Rab really means.

"I would like to find what he knows about the trial date for Parini, the person who killed Marcilene's husband. He might know something about the kidnapping trial dates for Hugo Verga and the girl."

"What a shame that a young girl would be caught up in such a deliberate crime."

"I know, Mom; she was probably brainwashed and coerced by her boyfriend."

CHAPTER FORTY-NINE

At the fishing village in Florida, three criminals, including the one escaped Vinni Peche, are plotting their next scheme. Vinni is determined to find and eliminate Minotti and Chiabrera. He must find Jennifer Aldrich and use her for a bargaining tool. If she is the daughter of either, they will come forward to save her. He has deviated into an erratic, eccentric mode more dangerous than ever. He actually has it in his mind that if he succeeds, he will be protected by the Sicilian mob. What he fails to realize through his reckless intelligence and overwhelming conceit, vindictive of most criminal minds, is the fact the authorities have knowledge of possible hideouts and of his contacts that may be called upon to help him. All are quickly put under surveillances. Hicks and Claudy are not easily recognized as wanted felons and go about freely to buy supplies, posing as fishermen on vacation. The newspapers in Miami make no note of the escape, leaving Vinni and the others to be a little more relaxed. However, the two women known as Peche's girlfriends are being watched carefully. The girlfriend known to have had a bartending job at Coconut Grove is traced to another location in Naples, Florida.

CHAPTER FIFTY

Rain is coming down in torrents in the city of London as Jennifer and David wait for Mr. Gates to join them in the library of his home. "How do you do? I am Winton Gates; what can I do for you?" A distinguished gentleman appearing to be in his sixties entered the room. Dressed in a maroon smoking jacket with a matching paisley ascot, he possessed a sense of propriety and refinement. "Mr. Gates, thank you for seeing us; my name is David Barr. I am a friend of Ms. Aldrich. I spoke briefly to you on the phone concerning Ms. Aldrich's mother, Dr. Janelle Aldrich."

"Yes, of course. As I explained to you, Dr. Aldrich was a dear friend of my brother. My dear, you have my deepest condolences. Your mother was a special person. She and my brother had a wonderful relationship when he was in the United States, before you were born. They continued to be friends until she was taken from us."

"Mr. Gates, your brother's name appears on my birth certificate as being my father. Is he, sir, my father?"

"Please, let us sit and visit; William will bring tea." A few moments of intense waiting and small talk by Canfield Gates seemed like an eternity to Jennifer. Tea and cakes were served by William, who then vanished from the room.

"My dear, sweet young woman, my brother would have been honored to be your biological father. However, my brother and your mother shared more of an intellectual relationship. They never shared an intimacy that would have brought you into this world."

"Then, with all due respect, sir, why does his name appear on my birth certificate?"

"Your mother had a brief but very meaningful relationship with a colleague of mine and dear friend of Winston's in the United States. Since they are both deceased, I feel that you are entitled to know. My brother was killed in Kuwait while working for the American government.

"Your biological father was married with a family. At the time, we felt it necessary to avoid a scandal that would have ruined his marriage and for no reason. At the time before your birth, your mother was going through some major changes in her life. She had a failed relationship with a colleague and was distraught. Our friend's wife became seriously ill; he was devastated. The two of them became a comfort to one another. When our friend's wife made a miraculous recovery, your mother moved to another state. It was a mutual agreement and worked out well, until your mother found out she had become pregnant. She confided in Winston the day you were born. He convinced her to list his name as your father to protect all concerned. It was a long time before she confessed to your father that he indeed had a small little girl named Jennifer. He was overjoyed and kept in touch with your mother; he followed all your accomplishments and became an important and supporting figure in your life. The two of them enjoyed a distant relationship after that and always took pride in the little girl they had together."

"Thank you, sir!"

"I hope this clears up things for you, dear."

"It does, all but the identity of my father."

"Before I go on, it would pleasure me a great deal if the two of you

114

would be our guests at a small dinner party that William and I are hosting tomorrow evening."

Both David and Jen listened intently as Mr. Canfield Gates was about to reveal the name of the man who became Jennifer Aldrich's biological father. The relief of knowing the truth quickly became obscured by the alarming facts. David, realizing that Jen is in extreme possible danger, decides he must be more protective.

The two overwhelmingly said their goodbyes and walked out into the rain before entering a waiting cab. Both are silent. Upon returning to the hotel, they agreed that to divulge what they learned could not be of benefit and vowed not to repeat the acquired knowledge from Mr. Gates—at least not for the time being. Tomorrow is another day and David plans to show Jen some more of England before they return home.

CHAPTER FIFTY-ONE

The morning is unusually bright, with no sign of rain clouds. During breakfast in the hotel dining room, the two of them break their silence and discuss the visit with Canfield Gates. "Are you sorry we came?"

"No! I just wish I had known more about my mother."

"Jen, your mother went to great lengths to protect you and to protect those lives that would have been affected by the truth."

"It is just hard to comprehend and get used to. This knowledge has given me a new family to think about."

"I assure you, it will all work out."

Jennifer gazes into space for a moment. "Jen, it is time to have some fun. We are going to visit the Wallace Museum first and then find a nice place for lunch." She smiles as she thinks how easily David can create a diversion. After the trip to the museum, they visited Westminster Abbey and saw where Princess Diana's funeral was held. "The Abbey is a living church that enshrines the history of the British Nation. Almost all the monarchs of England have been crowned in the Abbey. Some are buried next to the High Altar. The chapels are filled with colorful memorials."

They went through the Tower of London, her Majesty's palace and fortress, and saw the Crown Jewels. After a short trip on the River

Thames, they ate lunch at a British pub before going to St. Paul's Cathedral. They went by Parliament and saw where Margaret Thatcher had lived at Number Ten Downey Street. The present prime minister, Tony Blair, lives at Number Eleven Downey Street, as his family required larger quarters.

It was an exhausting day and agreeing to attend the dinner party didn't give them much time to rest before William Gates picked them up at 7:00 p.m.

It is an interesting party. Four out of six people are introduced to Jennifer and David as having met Dr. Aldrich; two were close friends and anxious to meet her daughter. Barry is a delicately handsome gentleman appearing younger than the others, even with a full head of white hair. Manfred, along with his wife, Elizabeth, is very talkative and entertaining. They knew Jennifer's mother quite well, having delightful stories to reveal. Manfred reminded Jennifer of a more slightly built and a little more handsome Alfred Hitchcock. James is a Walter-Mathou-type and verbally against the present White House administration. He curiously seemed eager to get that across to the Americans. Both Canfield and William Gates, being the gracious hosts, diplomatically changed the subject as quickly as possible. After all, you don't go to England and trash the queen.

The meal prepared by Helen was superbly presented. As tired as they should have been after such a long day, David and Jennifer found themselves not wanting the evening to end.

Having planned one more day to spend in London before leaving for the states, David insisted Jen sleep in the next morning and rest up for another sightseeing afternoon. The morning rain ended in time to walk out and eat brunch at a café bar on Albermarle Street; one street over is Bond Street where they visited the statues of Roosevelt and Churchill. Before the end of the day, they took a tour of Buckingham Palace. It is the summer opening of the state rooms at the official residences of the queen. The palace is furnished with works of art assembled over four centuries.

Dinner at Shino's Italian Restaurant, located in the Riverside Building County Hall on Westminster Bridge Road next to Dali's Museum, is a great finale, looking across the Thames facing Big Ben.

They both are reluctantly looking forward to the trip home the next day. David did everything possible to entertain Jen and was still able to complete his business at Scotland Yards.

Chapter Fifty-Two

The flight to Atlanta took eight and one-half hours. The last couple hours, they experienced a lot of shifting about, during an errant wind which Jennifer didn't find entertaining. However, with David by her side, she felt a tremendous calm.

Upon deplaning in Macon, the two are met by Special Agent Tilford. There was a brief update on Vinni Peche on the trip to Middleton and to Jennifer's condo. Marsha and Fox came out to greet them. "It's good to see my favorite roommate."

"It is good to see you also, Jennifer." David and Agent Tilford said their goodbyes.

"Jen, I will contact you in the morning. Try and get some rest. We are taking care of everything and I don't want you to worry about Vinni Peche."

"How was the trip?"

"Marsha, it was wonderful. David is an excellent tour guide and did everything in his power to occupy my mind. I was so happy about seeing London with him. We have gotten closer and I find myself depending on him too much."

"What do you mean?"

"Just that I am fortunate to have him in my life. I am just as fortunate to have you in my life. You have been like a sister I always dreamed of having."

"Well, sister, I have some news that I want to share and a question to ask."

"Oh?"

"Art and I have decided to get married in October and I want you to be my maid of honor." The two embrace and for a moment, neither thinks about the dangers threatening Jennifer.

"I am so happy for both of you. I would be delighted and honored."

"Good, maybe we will have time next week to go shopping. I would like your help in selecting a wedding gown."

In the morning, David's call was short and sweet. He professed what a wonderful time he had in London and how he would like to have had the time to show Paris to her. "There are no major developments in Vinni's capture, but we are close to knowing his whereabouts."

David returned Rab's call the next day to find he is in surgery and unavailable at present. "Mrs. Bharne, just tell him I have returned from England and am anxious to talk to him."

"I will, Mr. Barr; he has spoken to me of you and what admiration he has for the work you do."

"Thank you, I assure you, the feeling is mutual."

CHAPTER FIFTY-THREE

At the Isle of Capri, Vinni is preparing his next move. He is convinced Jennifer Aldrich has access to important documents that her mother was hiding, which may tell the location of Chiabrera or Minotti. His informant leads him to believe that Dr. Aldrich was treating the aftermath of facial reconstruction after they were placed in the witness protection program. He also believes, through an informant, that an ongoing intimate relationship was occurring between Dr. Aldrich and one of the two. His obsession with killing both men is increased.

"Claudy, I want you to take a trip to Middleton, Georgia; find out all you can about this woman, Jennifer Aldrich. Stay in contact with me! Hicks, you're too scary-looking to go. I need you to stay here, buy supplies, and keep me in touch with the news."

In Central America, bordering Yucatan, Mexico, and Guatemala in Belize, news reaches Hector Gonzalez that a thug by the name of Vinni Peche has escaped and is on the run from law enforcement. It is believed he is a danger to two men in seclusion known formerly as Giacomo Minotti and Luigi Chiabrera.

Hector, a narcotics wholesaler transformed into a secret confidential informant for the United States and having knowledge of the whereabouts of both men, promptly sailed to Ambergis Caye, an island below the Yucatan, close to the Belize border, where he met with Minotti, whom he knew and referred to as Vincent Carlos. "Vince, you must take precautions. This man is desperate to gain recognition by the Sicilian mob. He is on a mission and will not stop."

"I will be careful. Thank you for coming. I will be coming back to Belize to take care of some business; I will check in with you; keep your ears open."

Belize is in close proximity to the United States and has a strong trade relationship with the United Kingdom. Natural resources help promote the tourism market. Vincent Carlos and his partner, Aldo Tripoli, legitimate businessmen, are in the import-export business. "In 2000, the United States accounted for 48.5 percent of Belize's total exports and provided 49.7 percent of all Belizean imports." Belize continues to rely on foreign trade with the United States, although manufacturing agro-products and tourism are primary sectors of the economy.

Water and electricity are plentiful, but roads are of poor quality, preventing industry from having easy access.

One of the factors working against the Belizean government is the involvement in the South American drug trade. Hector Gonzalez has been an asset in helping alleviate some of the drug problems. He and the two men, Vincent and Aldo, having become good friends and confidants to a degree, are keeping a low profile and continuing to be protective of one another.

CHAPTER FIFTY-FOUR

It has been a few years since Giacomo Miontti lost contact with his family. He was devastated when his daughter was murdered. He blames himself because of an earlier affiliation with the mob. Since his facial surgery, name change, and new business, he has led a crime-free life along with his partner, "Aldo Tripoli," previously known as Luigi Chiabrera. The two testified against several Sicilian mobsters in exchange for the lifestyles to which they have adapted. However, two of the persons against whom they testified avoided capture and suffering the consequences. They are believed to be living in exile out of the United States. These crime figures are well organized and protected by family and members of their organization; most are related in some way to other members; they will never give up looking for the informants who sold them out and caused their brothers to serve prison terms and be given death sentences. Vinni Peche hopes to help by getting to them first.

Luigi, now known as Aldo Tripoli, was divorced long before his crime spree ended. Without siblings or children left behind, he has an easier time adjusting to a new life. The two of them have enjoyed spending a sufficient amount of time in Ambergris Caye for the laid-back atmosphere. The island is close to the barrier reef that runs by Cozumel. Snorkeling and diving have become avid interests for both.

Having been on the road taking his sweet time for a day and a half, Claudy is making his way to fulfill his mission for his boss. He arrives in Middleton at dusk, checks into a small bed-and-breakfast, and starts making inquires of the proprietor about the town and neighborhoods. He asks about the hospital, crime rate, etc., pretending to be interested in settling down and finding work. The conversation led to the recent murders of the Panacheks and to the assassination of a prominent physician several years prior. He expresses false concern and appears passive as the woman behind the desk reminds him that the town is virtually crime-free, but for those two terrible tragedies. He pleasantly asks for a local telephone book and retires to a small sleeping room overlooking the main street.

The following day, Claudy visits Jennifer's neighborhood and notices a for-sale sign posted in front of a condo. He wastes no time in calling the realtor, who is delighted to have someone interested in the property where the whole town knows a double murder had occurred. He started asking about the neighborhood and about people living in the area. The realtor gave him a complete run-down of each of the occupants available to her, including a young nurse living next door who works at the local Memorial Hospital. Claudy, turning away and expressing a beatific smile, thanked the agent and promised to get back in touch. Overjoyed with thinking he is able to pick up useful information, he reports back to Peche. "I want you to track this woman's every move. Find out if she lives alone, her working hours, who her friends are. I want what's on her birth certificate. *Capisci?*"

"Okay! Vinni, I'll get it done."

CHAPTER FIFTY-FIVE

Through coordination with colleagues in international investigations and the efforts of the FBI to protect Americans, David obtained information leading to the necessity of locating Minotti and Chiabrera. It is the goal of the FBI's international presence to stop crime as far from American soil as possible and to help solve international crimes as quickly as possible. There are over fifty small legal attaché offices (Legats) in US embassies and consulates around the world. The legal attaché program is overseen by the office of International Operations, headed by a special agent in charge at FBI headquarters in Washington, DC. The Legats keep in close contact with Interpol and other federal agencies and are critical to an effort to help FBI in global crime. Interpol serves as a clearinghouse of information and is equipped to provide information on matters dealing with worldwide criminal activity, but has no law-enforcement powers. The FBI has a broad jurisdiction.

Each country has a specialty of crime. The Australians pickpocket all over the world. The Indians do airline ticket schemes; Russians, organized crime; Italians are known for organized crime, violence, kidnapping, and extortion; the French, economic espionage; while Japan organizes gangs.

Armed with classified information on the whereabouts of Minotti and Chiabrera, David boards a plane in Atlanta in route to Miami and then to Belize. It has become imperative for him to talk to these people and make them aware of dangers that have become eminent. Entry into Belize will be relatively simple, as visas are not required of the United States, Canada, or the European Union member nations.

Belize is a country of various cultures. Due to racial harmony and religious tolerance, Belize has gained a widespread reputation for its friendly people. Approximately 270,000 people in Belize consist of the Creole, Garifuna, Spanish, Maya, English, Mennonite, Lebanese, Chinese, and East Indian. One of the most prominent ethnic groups is Creoles, descendants of early British settlers with African slaves.

Visitors are permitted to stay in Belize for a period of thirty days, unless an extension is granted through San Pedro, Punta Gorda, Belmopan, or Orange Walk.

CHAPTER FIFTY-SIX

It is 10:00 a.m. when David's plane touched down at the Philip S. Goldson International Airport, ten miles from Belize City in Ladyville. The weather is sixty-eight degrees. The sub-tropical climate is tempered by trade winds. Rain is pretty steady. The dry season that usually starts in February and continues to the end of May has yet to begin.

The cab driver is extremely informative. He points out the characteristics of his country, the economics, government officials, etc. "The queen of Belize has been Elizabeth II since 1952. The board of directors is run by the governor and vice chairman of the bank of Belize. The Belize dollar is the official currency, divided into one hundred cents. One USD is worth two BZD. The government is divided into three branches: the executive, legislative, and judicial. No elections take place. The monarch is heredity. The monarch appoints the governor general and the governor appoints the prime minister."

The lesson is quite interesting to David, who wondered why this seemingly highly intelligent resident is a cab driver. "Sir, where did you get your education?"

"I studied in Europe and the United States. I guess you might say I am a dedicated student. I love the atmosphere here, the people, and all the cultures. Back in the states, I had a position as professor of Arts and Sciences at Harvard. This is the lifestyle I want. I have never been happier."

"I am amazed and, in a lot of ways, very envious. Do you have family?"

"Yes, I have a wife here with me. Our two sons are in New York. One is an investment banker, the other a Philadelphia attorney."

"Sir, you are amazing!" David shakes his hand as he departs the cab at the Holiday Inn. "I am very happy to have made your acquaintance."

Upon entering the hotel, David is aware of his surroundings and cautiously admits to the desk clerk he is on a holiday. A private company, Belize Telecommunications Limited, owns the automatic telephone service that covers the entire country. David brought his own phone with him and activated it at BTL's airport location.

He wasted no time in contacting the import-export company owned by Aldo Tripoli and Vincent Carlos. Pretending to be a tourist looking into the business of exporting, he was able to schedule a meeting with Carlos at 4:00 p.m. He was greeted at 3:35 p.m. by a young friendly Hispanic woman, and asked to wait for just a moment as she disappeared through a closed door with an obvious coded security system. David was aware he was being watched through a two-way mirrored glass on the wall behind the receptionist's desk. When she returned, she invited him to follow her to Mr. Carlos's office. She returned to her desk.

CHAPTER FIFTY-SEVEN

"Mr. Carlos, I have come under false pretense. My name is Special Agent David Barr with the FBI. I have come from the United States to have a meeting with you and your partner." Vincent Carlos nervously opened his desk drawer.

"May I see your identification?"

"Of course, sir. Forgive me. I had to make sure you are alone."

"What business do you have with me or my partner?"

"First, I must tell you that my father was Dr. Avery Barr. His murder was never solved. This is not why I have come. We have reason to believe that you and your partner are in danger of being exposed and may have to change identity and location."

"Agent Barr," he said, closing his desk drawer, "I am aware of Vinni Peche and his want-to-be claim to fame."

"He is a threat, but I assure you, we are not intimidated. There is a greater threat than Peche. I would like very much to talk to the two of you as soon as possible. As you know, it would not be wise to talk about the content of our meeting to anyone. I am staying at the Holiday Inn. Please call me as soon as this is possible."

"I will talk to my partner."

David opened the door to leave. "Thank you, Mr. Carlos, for your time. I hope we will be able to do a little export business sometime in the future."

It took two days for Aldo Tripoli and Vincent Carlos to validate Special Agent David Barr's legitimacy. They set up a meeting in the evening at the company after all other employees departed. The three of them sat down as David began bringing them up-to-date on some of the events surrounding the murders of Minotti's daughter Elizabeth, and Anthony Panachek.

"Two people from Palermo that you testified against several years ago are dedicated to finding your identity before they are executed. They have vowed to make an example and are making this known through relatives in Sicily. Our communicant has knowledge of a group devoted to carrying out these threats as a sign of honor. To them, it is like a worship of deity to a sacred purpose. These individuals are perceived to be legendary martyrs."

"What information do you believe they have?"

"We are taking every precaution to prevent them from developing knowledge of your identities. My purpose for being here is to make you aware to be prepared to leave immediately if they gain momentum. Until we can know more about this situation, I will be your only contact with our agency. We will define a code of cipher intelligence between us while the authorities continue to sabotage this threat."

"Is there an immediate reason for us to leave?"

"No, Mr. Tripoli, but whenever an expression of retaliation is a potential source, there is a menacing indication of danger. The mobsters who avoided capture during the trials in which you testified have been located and are within our reach. It is through observation focused on these individuals that made us conscious of some alarming facts concerning your safety. We are reserving time, gathering information before moving in."

CHAPTER FIFTY-EIGHT

"Agent Barr, Mr. Tripoli and I want to tell you how sorry we are about the deaths of your father and the lady doctor. We regret having been the cause. If we could help in providing information to solve the crime, we would."

"Thank you, Mr. Carlos. For a time, I wasn't sure it wasn't carried out by you. I now have knowledge to betray that theory."

"Your father was a good man and a friend to us, as well as Dr. Jan, of whom we were very fond. It is a tragedy we will never forget."

"I will be leaving soon. Are there any questions before we plan our signals of communication?"

"No!" they said in unison. After a brief indoctrination into the world of law-abiding deceit, the two men said goodbye to Special Agent David Barr, leaving him to his thoughts of how two intelligent, educated men could have been attracted to a life of crime.

"Fortunately for those two, they have repented for their involvement with the mob and are living a good life. At least for now."

Back at the fishing camp on the Isle of Capri in Florida, Hicks is recognizable by his tainted complexion and unpleasant looks. A golfer on vacation from Chicago remembers him as someone who was wanted for aiding in the escape of a prisoner. A couple of calls are made and

Hicks is taken into custody. He refuses to give up the location of Vinni. He is questioned at the Naples police department by a beefy man with an Irish brogue. "I don't know where Vinni is. I left him in Atlanta."

"What about Claudy? Where did you leave him?"

"I dropped them both off at the same time. They are probably gambling in one of the casinos."

"Read him his rights and lock him up."

"I want to call my attorney," he yells as he is being processed and fingerprinted.

Vinni is nervously anxious for Hicks to return. When he doesn't show up all night, Vinni calls Middleton, Georgia. "Claudy, what can you tell me about Hicks? Does he have friends in Florida? He has disappeared."

"I don't know, Vinni. He is pretty loyal to his friends, but none I know are in Florida. How long has he been gone?"

"Overnight!"

"I wouldn't put too much stock in his leaving, at least for another day. He may have taken up with some broad. He has been known to do that from time to time."

"Okay, what have you got for me there?"

"I found out this nurse you asked me to check out is pretty tight with an FBI Agent. They just spent a week in London together. She is back at work and he is out of town."

"Good, this is an opportunity for you to get acquainted with her. Make her like you and trust you."

"Okay, Vinni, I'll do my best."

"Just do it!"

CHAPTER FIFTY-NINE

David's plane touched down at the Miami International Airport at 5:17 p.m. Upon reaching the Delta Crown room, he places a call to his new friend, Rab. "Do you have time for dinner before your connection?"

"Yes, indeed I do. My flight does not leave for three hours."

"Good, I will pick you up."

"Thanks, Rab, that will be great." After a brief cocktail at Rab's home with his mother, the two leave for dinner at a popular Italian restaurant not far from the airport.

"How is Jennifer?"

"She is doing fine. The two of us recently went to London. I had some business to take care of at Scotland Yard, and she wanted to follow up on some new information about her mother and father."

"Oh, I see. Was she able to find anything credible?"

"Yes, as a matter of fact, we were both stunned by the identification of her father, which came from someone living in London who was close to the situation. I am not at liberty to divulge his identity at this time, merely to protect those that could be affected. How have you been, and how is your significant other?"

Rab, looking surprised, chuckles. "I beg your pardon, I am unaware

I have a significant other."

"Jennifer is under the assumption that you are having a serious relationship with a nurse. She saw a picture of you on two occasions in the society column of the *Miami Herald*."

"So that's the reason for the cold letter I received from her. It was almost like a Dear John. Well, that particular nurse is or was a co-worker of mine. She had season tickets to the theatre, which I enjoy. I attended a few performances with her after having taken her to dinner. She wanted more than a casual relationship, and when she all but stalked me, I arranged for a transfer for her to another department."

After a long pause, David said, "Rab, why not get in touch with Jennifer and clear this up?"

"It seems to me it is a little late; aren't you and Jennifer an item?"

"I love Jennifer, but we are not an item. The trip to London was strictly business. We traveled together. We did not stay together. I have a suggestion: I am so sure of the reception you will get from her that I want to invite you to a wedding next month for a couple agent friends of ours." Smiling, Rab cannot say yes soon enough. "Good, it is all set then. I won't say anything to her; just show up. I will give you all the details."

CHAPTER SIXTY

Dropping him off at the departure gate, Rab shakes David's hand. "You don't know what this visit has meant to me. Thank you, David." The two are now conniving brothers.

When David returned to Middleton, he called on Jen and Marsha. He did not mention his dinner engagement with Rab. "David, I ran into a man today who asked me to dinner."

"What do you mean you ran into him?"

"I physically ran into this man as I was leaving the hospital. He was looking down and stumbled into me. He struck up a conversation and eventually asked me out."

"What did you say?"

"I told him I wasn't free to date, but thank you."

"Good answer. What did this man look like?"

"He had dark hair, graying at the temples, and looked to be around forty or forty-five, with hazel eyes. He was about five-foot-ten, dressed in a blue shirt and dark trousers, no tie."

"Now that is a thorough description. I will make a law enforcement officer of you after all. I want you to be aware of this man and let me know if you see him again. In my line of work, I am leery about chance encounters."

"Okay, David, I promise." Turning to Marsha, she said, "He has become my great protector."

"Jen, David is right; please let either of us know if you see this man again."

"By the way, Marsha, when is this great event taking place?"

"In three weeks. Jen and I are going on a shopping trip to Macon this weekend to look for gowns. She is going to be my maid of honor."

"That sounds good, just be careful of your surroundings."

CHAPTER SIXTY-ONE

Once again, Vinni is on the phone. "Claudy, he still hasn't shown. I am concerned that maybe he was picked up and will spill his guts."

"I'm telling you, Vinni, he has picked up some woman. He'll be back when he gets tired of her. I have seen him do this before. I made a connection with the nurse. She was friendly and I am going to try again to take her out. That's the most positive news I can give you at this time."

"All right, go for it and do not fail. I want to know if she has a safety deposit box. Anything you can grab onto. If you have to, grab her, shake her up, tie her up, and force it out."

Now Claudy knows he is unable to get all this information from someone he doesn't even know without force, but the money that Vinni has promised him is a good incentive to try. He decides to stall Vinni one more day. If nothing materializes, he will have to use harsher tactics. After all, he is not above kidnapping, extortion, or violence.

The trip to Macon proved to be eventful for Marsha and Jen. Marsha chose a simple white satin gown, trimmed in velvet, elegant in design, with a net veil attached to a small but classy matching velvet hat. Jen's dress is ankle-length soft velvet, plain in design, form-fitting, in a delicate color of reddish yellow. The gowns justify the time of year as

October is approaching. The two are so pleased with themselves they decide to have a drink to celebrate, have dinner at their hotel, and shop for shoes the next day.

Claudy is almost in a rage looking for Jennifer. "What will I tell Vinni? I have lost her trail for two days. She hasn't been home or at the hospital." Positioning himself close to her residence, he waits through Saturday night. Finally, Sunday afternoon he makes a point to check again and sees her get out of a car with another woman. They have two small bags of luggage, carrying parcels and dress bags. The two enter Jennifer's condo. Now all he has to do is wait until the other woman leaves. She does not leave. The lights go out at 10:00 p.m. Claudy decides it is useless and goes back to his room to try to catch her alone when she goes to work the next morning. He has staked out a vacant building, preparing to take her there, bind her, and get all the information he can, however he can. He is desperate. This has lingered longer than he intended; Vinni is restless and he must get back to try to locate Hicks.

The next morning at 6:30 a.m., when Jennifer leaves for the hospital, he is waiting. The street is quiet and dark. He crouches down beside her car and waits for her to approach. Just as she reaches out to unlock and open the door, he lunges for her in a ruthless manner. His arm tightened around her throat; she loses consciousness as he tosses her into the back seat of her car like a sack of potatoes. When he leans back to get into the driver's seat, picking her keys up off the floor of the car, a dark figure grabs his head, slams him to the pavement, and waits for Marsha to apply the handcuffs. An ambulance is called, along with back-up to take him to the city jail. The two of them showed little mercy in restraining him. His jaw is broken and his nose is bleeding profusely. He is not afforded the luxury of an ambulance. The back-up car sped off with Claudy in the back, dazed, bleeding, stupefied, and bewildered, in shock of what just happened. How could he have been detected?

David rode in the ambulance with Jennifer, while Marsha gave a description to the local police about the turn of events. Again, the neighbors were aghast at all the commotion. Marsha assured them everything was all right. "Just an attempted burglary. The police were following him."

In the ambulance, Jennifer is given oxygen before she awakened to see her guardian angel. "David, what happened?"

"You had a stalker. Marsha and I decided to take some extra precautions after you reported that a man had inadvertently bumped into you. She noticed someone in a parked car down the street from your home when the two of you returned from Macon. The car left after your lights were turned off. Let's just say I had a feeling and decided it was worth checking to see if he returned, so I have been in the shadows all night while Marsha watched from the window. What do you remember?"

"I was grabbed from behind and everything went black. I don't remember anything after that. I don't think I'm hurt." Her voice quivered in disbelief. "Where is the stalker now?"

"He should be at police headquarters about now, wiping blood off his face. We'll have him in a line-up tomorrow. Right now, I want to have you checked out at the hospital, and if you are okay, I will take you home." David answers his cell phone.

"Yes, Marsha, we are still in the emergency room, but with the exception of a few bruises and being shaken she will be fine, thanks to your good judgment and police work. I should be bringing her back soon." Jennifer looks admiringly toward David as he puts his phone into his pocket.

"David, you are too good to me."

"Don't ever forget you are special to me. Didn't you save my life?"

CHAPTER SIXTY-TWO

The next day, Marsha accompanies Jennifer to the police line-up, where she identifies her attacker as the man whom she thought accidentally bumped into her a few days earlier. His fingerprints are being sent for a comparison to one Claudy Estes.

Claudy's telephone continues to ring in Detective Raymore's office. No one answers while the calls are traced to Florida. The phone number is listed through a company name, which proves to be bogus. The authorities are confident they have their man Claudy, but will wait for conclusive evidence.

Jennifer explained to the hospital administrator that she was detained because of an encounter with a burglary suspect in her neighborhood. Mark Powers, concerned about her, detects that she is one calm and cool lady with the confidence to do her job. He approaches a couple of times during her shift and is amazed at how well she handles herself after such an ordeal.

After all, she is getting pretty good about accepting crime-induced chaos as part of her life.

The fingerprint results have verified that Claudy Estes, a known criminal wanted in connection with the escape of Vinni Peche, is the person in custody. Both Hicks and Claudy have been apprehended and are being processed for extradition to Chicago. "Vinni is running out of time," David says to himself.

Two days later, the *Chicago Tribune* printed the story:

TWO ACCOMPLICES HARBORING ESCAPEE VINNI PECHE IN CUSTODY

The two men accused of helping Peche escape from the Chicago Justice Center on September 11 have been apprehended by police without incident. Vinni Peche, believed to be in the Florida area and heavily armed, is wanted by the FBI.

Vinni, aware that his two cohorts are not going to be of any help, still allowing he is invincible and can outsmart the law for which he has an incredible contempt, begins to plan his next strategy. He mentally considered contacting one of his girlfriends, but then aborts that idea, deciding she may be under the watchful eye of the law. One thing is for sure: he will have to leave his present location in case Hicks or Claudy decides to talk.

CHAPTER SIXTY-THREE

Meanwhile, word has reached Danny Marino, a *solon* or lawmaker of the Sicilian mafioso in Palermo, that one Vinni Peche, a Chicago mobster with former family ties to Sicily, is out to make history and may have knowledge of the whereabouts of Minotti and Chiabrera. "What a break this could be after ten years of searching."

"I don't know, Danny!" doubts his cousin, Junie.

"If Peche is on the run in Florida, he can be found through our contacts in Miami. Go down there and get the word out that we can help him. He'll surface when he gets desperate. The rumor is that he is running out of hideouts."

"Okay, Danny, I could stand a little change of scenery."

Junie Poeta is a middle-aged, muscular, and moderately handsome man, rough and hearty in manner. He is charismatic when the opportunity falls to his advantage and known by his peer group to be unequalled in acts of violence. He is frequently called upon as a "cleaner." A master of disguises, he can appear and go non-descriptively undetected.

The search for Peche was underway before Junie deplaned at Miami International Airport. A plan is put meticulously into effect by the underworld contacts known to Danny Marino. Junie quickly went to a phone booth and dialed a number given him by his cousin.

He then went to the rental car counter, after which he entered a small SUV and proceeded to meet with his contact.

Back in Chicago, the court-appointed attorneys for both Claudy and Hicks advised them to hope for a plea bargain and give up information of their last location. The two didn't need much persuading. Hicks, proclaiming his innocence in the escape plot for Vinni, delivered an almost musical version of his role in aiding a wanted criminal, eager to implicate others. Claudy, on the other hand, with a mental grasp on the circumstances of his capture, would have sold out his mother to save his skin. The two defendants separately made appeals for light sentences, claiming they had been seduced into doing something, and they now claim to have been stupid and shown poor judgment on their parts. In the end, the judge would not be lenient.

The fishing camp at the Isle of Capri is promptly invaded by law enforcement officers. Signs of having been vacated hurriedly produced clues, some thought to be important; most of them proved unimposing.

Chapter Sixty-Four

At 10:00 p.m., Sunday, September 16, the phone rang in the bedroom of Jennifer Aldrich's condominium. It is late afternoon in London when the voice of Canfield Gates took on a note of urgency. Identifying himself, he cautiously asks to speak to Jennifer. "Hello, Mr. Gates, how are you? This is Jennifer."

"Jennifer, I must tell you, I have been going through some of my late brother's belongings and have discovered a dossier belonging to your mother. The envelope is sealed and appears to have several documents inside. The note attached asks Winston to keep the folder for safekeeping. The folder went unnoticed until now, as my brother left several manuscripts and documents yet to be examined." Her heart racing with excitement, Jennifer pleads with Mr. Gates to please keep the envelope until she talks to David.

"Thank you so much for your call, Mr. Gates. David will know how best to obtain the folder. I am forever grateful and will be in touch soon. Please say hello to William."

"David, I know it's late but I must talk to you about a telephone call from Mr. Gates moments ago."

Realizing the emotion in her voice, David said, "Jen, I don't know how safe our telephone conversation can be; I will be right over."

"Thank you, David! Marsha is out with Art and I desperately want to talk to you."

Thirty minutes dragged by before she heard David's footsteps. She runs to the door. "Oh! David," she said as they embrace. She blurts out the entire conversation with Canfield Gates. "Jennifer, don't get your hopes up, but I suspect the information in that folder is pretty important or your mother wouldn't have made this kind of effort to protect its contents. I will sleep on this and phone London tomorrow to make arrangements to have it flown here. I'll call Mr. Gates and let him expect what I think will be the safest transfer."

"Do you think I will finally have closeness to my mother's past?"

"I suspect you very well may. Now, I know you are understandably tapping on the hive, but you must curb your excitement, and get a good night's sleep. I will call you tomorrow." Amused by his expression of her excitement, Jennifer walks David to the door before calmly reading herself to sleep. She does not hear the door when Marsha returns.

The next day, David made contact with Scotland Yard and arranged for a courier to pick up the dossier from Mr. Gates. After they enjoyed dinner at Eva Barr's residence, Mrs. Barr said goodnight to David, Jen, and Marsha before retiring to her quarters.

"Jen, I have news. I felt under the circumstances the contents of your mother's well-guarded documents should be reviewed by me. I hope you don't mind."

"No, of course not, David. I trust you with everything I have."

"Good! Considering the value of some of the papers I have viewed by satellite, a courier will arrive in two days, delivering the entire package to me. I would like for us to go over it together."

"David what is in the package?"

"There are pictures of your childhood, documents from her practice, her findings and thoughts about my father's death, and the fears she had for you and her own life. I found her to be a remarkable woman and you will also. There is also a lockbox key belonging to a bank here in Middleton. The box is paid for several years in advance. It is registered to Janelle and Jennifer Aldrich."

"I don't understand all this, David; the more we find out, the more of a mystery it is."

"I know it seems that way, but it will come together."

CHAPTER SIXTY-FIVE

A call received the following day by FBI headquarters from a woman in Cincinnati not giving her name but insisting she is the sister of Vinni Peche was relayed to Agent David Barr. The woman claimed her brother called, asking for help to find a place for him to stay in Cincinnati. She stated she did not hesitate to deny any help to him. After apologizing to the agent for all the problems caused by her brother, she gave the number on her caller ID from which the call had come. The phone number was traced to a pay phone along a beach area in Ft. Lauderdale, Florida.

After confirming the call from the woman is a legitimate call from one of Peche's sisters living in Cincinnati, a unit was quickly sent to Ft. Lauderdale to stake out the area. Two undercover agents posing as beach bums are two of the unit members combing the area, keeping a watchful eye on a particular telephone. Further surveillance yielded a dead end.

Peche, fearing his sister had called the authorities, entered the rental car with Tennessee license plates and drove back toward Miami. He registered at a small motel close to Hollywood under an alias of Carl Mori. It didn't take long for him to become acquainted with a thirty-six-year-old recent divorcee named Jane Belmont, who would become a female companion. The two met at the Tiki Bar behind the motel, located in the area between the pool and the beach. He told her he was an undercover police officer looking for an escapee believed to be in Hollywood. She, being vulnerable to temptation, is impressed and offered to be of assistance.

In the meantime, the word is out by the underworld to be on alert, watching for Vinni Peche, assumed traveling alone and could be anywhere in Miami or Ft. Lauderdale, or in between. The rental car he is thought to be driving, by a stroke of chance, was traced by an informant of the crime world at the Isle of Capri and seen once again in Ft. Lauderdale.

Vinni, or Carl as he is now called by his new friend Jane, has a new sense of security, spawning a freshly grown moustache, dyed reddish hair, tanned body, and a new wardrobe. He feels good about his ability to elude the authorities and confident enough to escort his friend out nightclubbing. "Life is improved. Vinni has outsmarted the law."

CHAPTER SIXTY-SIX

He may have cleverly dodged the law for now, but not the underground Mafia. They are hot on his trail and intend to find out what he knows about their prey and the murders of a decade ago. Is he able to tell them the location of the two who put their brothers behind bars to await execution? Does Vinni Peche know what really happened to Dr. Vogel? Can he implicate them in this unsolved crime? There are so many questions.

It has been just twenty-four hours since Junie Poeta arrived in Florida and met with Danny's contacts. He hastily started scanning the area hotels and motels one after another, looking for a Tennessee license plate on a rental car. He and his Miami counterparts asked questions in virtually every gas station along A1 or Confederate Highway, and along Collins Avenue. They visited the nightclub scene, which they thought he might frequent. They constantly showed his picture that had been displayed in the Chicago newspapers. Too many people were out to find Vinni. It is imperative they do so before the FBI.

Vinni decided it was time to get rid of the blue Chevrolet he had rented in Tennessee, now that he could obtain another without a trail. He left the car abandoned at the Ft. Lauderdale International Airport and waited for Jane, who is under the assumption he turned the car in for another, so he would not be noticed as an undercover. She obediently rented a Town Car in her name from another location and delivered it to him. "How good is this?" he thinks to himself. "She'll do anything I ask, without questions." Vinni, still having ample funds, is feeling pretty self-assured. His self-confidence is excelled by his newly formed identity and by his devoted companion he is able to skillfully coerce.

Poeta is well on the trail after having spotted the car left behind by Vinni at the airport. After identifying himself to the attendant as owner of the car rental company from which the car had been rented, he obtains the date and time the car had been left. Realizing Vinni might still be in the area, and probably close by, Poeta and some of his acquaintances from Miami continue showing his picture to motel clerks, centering along the beaches. Most criminals have something in common; for example, Junie Poeta likes the beach area, enjoys the night life, spending money, and acting like a big shot. However, he doesn't have a lot of respect for women, having grown up in an abusive foster home. Therefore, because of his distrust, he doesn't keep relationships with the opposite sex for long. Having covered most of the beach-front hotels from Ft. Lauderdale toward Haulover Beach, Junie and his crew decide to wait until the next day before continuing a search in Hollywood and Bal Harbor.

CHAPTER SIXTY-SEVEN

It is 2:00 p.m. on Sunday in Middleton when David arrives at Jennifer's door with the package received from London. It had arrived by courier two hours earlier. Jennifer is overwhelmed with anxiety as she opens the large envelope containing the dossier and photographs so carefully preserved by Dr. Janelle Aldrich. A sealed envelope addressed to Jennifer Aldrich is quickly opened as Jennifer reads with euphoria.

> *Dearest Jennifer,*
>
> *When you read this, I will be with you in spirit. I have lived a wonderful life, had many happy experiences, and been especially blessed with you for a daughter. You have been the light of my life. I only have to look at you to see all the wonder and beauty that life can bring. Your smile gives me all the joy of the world.*
>
> *I have made endless decisions in my lifetime, some good and a few regrets. There was never a moment that I didn't appreciate the fulfillment from the beautiful expression of love we have shared. May the love that surrounds you fill the void you are feeling and may you find understanding, comfort, and encouragement in the notes I have prepared.*

By this time you will know the true identity of your biological father. He is a man devoted to his wife and children. His love for his wife never faltered when she was so desperately ill. We were drawn together not by an affair, but by the emotions of two people sharing love for one another as friends, and were equally distraught over circumstances beyond control. Your father is a part of your life and cares for you very deeply. He is sometimes saddened by the emptiness of not having you closer to him. We continue to respect one other and enjoy a closeness that is above reproach.

There are documents in this package that are not to be exploited. I trust you to keep them safe and share them at your discretion in view of urgency by the government. There is a photograph album containing pictures of you, me, your father, and friends that have been close to us from the time you were born and through your young childhood.

A key is enclosed to a lock box with instructions of the location. Inside, you will find documents of my practice. Included is your legitimate birth certificate and pieces of jewelry kept for your graduation. The large sum of money enclosed is for you as a dowry.

Writing this to you at this time is to help give me a sense of completion. I cannot bear the thought of leaving you without confidence and hope. May the times shared together and the loving bonds between us fill the path of separation, whenever that will be. You have made my life complete.

Your loving mother

Jen shares the letter with David, who silently holds her close with an understanding heart.

The picture album displaying affection of both parents is of great importance to her and gives a much-needed closure to her bereavement. It is a comfort at a time of sadness.

"David, your love and acceptance have meant so much to me. I wouldn't have known where to turn without your help and friendship."

"Jen, you are important to me. I want us to always be close." There is a long pause.

"Are you ready to check out the lockbox?"

"Yes, Jen, if you don't mind, I want to review these documents at home before taking them to the office. They indicate a lot of reading about patients of your mother and my father."

"Of course, David, I want you to be in charge."

The bank manager is very cooperative at the Middleton branch of Commonwealth and Trust. Jennifer's signature is already on a signature card, preventing a problem. She had forgotten about signing the card at her mother's request, and at the time, was too young to question the reason.

She and David entered a safe room and prepared to discover the contents of box B60007 behind closed doors. "Wow!" David remarks. "There is a substantial amount of cash in this envelope by the weight of it." Several pieces of jewelry included a diamond necklace with an opal enhancer she had seen her mother wear. The opal was her mother's birthstone, as well as hers. A gift package with her birthstone ring and matching bracelet was opened. The bracelet was inscribed: "To Jennifer, my precious gem." There are also several journals kept by Dr. Aldrich.

After counting the money, David suggested she leave the money in the box for security before contacting a professional consultant for possible investment decisions. She decided to take some of the jewelry home with her. The stack of documents recovered were quickly turned over to David, who has particular interest. "Jen, I will take very good care of this documentation and will let you know my findings."

"Thank you, David. This has been one collective day. I hope these papers will give some insight as to what happened to both parents. I don't know about you, but I have the impression from Mother's letter to me that she was anticipating an early death and was frightened."

"Yes, I did get that impression as well. You may get more information after reading her diary from her journals."

"I plan to do that tonight."

"Your mother left quite a legacy."

CHAPTER SIXTY-EIGHT

A man enters the Sunlight Inn at dusk. It is a pleasant evening in Hollywood, Florida; the temperature is in the mid-seventies. A clerk just coming on duty is shown a photograph and recognizes a strong resemblance to one of the guests. Junie Poeta, cleverly concealed, is waiting when Carl and his companion arrive at 2:00 a.m. after an evening out. Poeta decided to wait until morning to approach and verify the identity of Vinni Peche.

With scrupulous circumspect, the hands of a skillfully trained criminal examined the contents of a white Lincoln recently parked at the motel. The glove compartment contained an invoice and agreement from a Fort Lauderdale rental agency, revealing the name of Jane Belmont, a resident of Sandusky, Ohio.

Junie loses little time in contacting his cousin Danny Moreno in Sicily. "I have traced Peche to Hollywood. He has modified his looks, but I'm sure it's him. He has a female companion. What do you want me to do?"

"Good work! Now get him alone, away from the woman. Gain his confidence; find out what he knows and if he is on the trail of Minotti and Chiabrera. I intend to make them pay if it takes another ten years."

Patience is of the essence now, as Poeta waits for the right time to strike up a conversation with Peche. He must be careful not to scare him into thinking the authorities are at his heels. At 10:30 a.m. the couple appears for brunch at the outside restaurant. "This is going to be harder than expected to get him alone." Finally, the woman disappears through the doors of the motel and a cleverly apt and simple scheme is contrived to become acquainted with Vinni Peche. As Junie passes the table, he trips, and in catching himself from what appeared to be a disastrous fall, spills a cup of very hot coffee on his target. "I'm very sorry, sir, are you hurt? I seemed to have lost my balance."

"My leg is burned." Two motel employees immediately appeared with a first aid kit. After applying a salve of aloe vera, Vinni continued to screech with pain. "Please, let me take you to a doctor." Junie seems sincere.

"There is a clinic not far from here; I will give you the address," the accommodating motel manger offers. Vinni, in agonizing pain, does not hesitate getting into the car.

"I regret causing such a bad burn. My name is Junie Poeta. I am a visitor from Sicily." Vinni, impressed by this person's heritage, exclaims, "My name is Carl Mori. I am on vacation from the Chicago area." The two exchange some knowledge of one another on the way to and from the clinic. The doctor at the clinic had given Carl a prescription for pain after he administered a salve to the burn.

"The lady I saw you with, is she your wife?"

"No, she is a friend."

"Will you be in Florida long?"

"I am not sure just how long. What about you?"

"I have business and will go back to Italy." Now Vinni is really intent on finding out more about this acquaintance from Sicily. Not wanting anyone to hear the name Peche since he is on the run, Vinni does not divulge information that his grandfather was an immigrant from the island of Sicily. The two continue their conversation out side in a lounge area close to the pool where Carl carefully props his leg on a chair. Jane, after expressing her concern over the accident, proceeds to go for a swim at the beach. She is not introduced to Mr. Poeta.

CHAPTER SIXTY-NINE

The next day, Junie prepares to get closer to the victim of his not-so-subtle introduction. "Hello, Carl, I am just calling to see how your burn is coming along."

"It seems to be better. The pain has lessened."

"That's wonderful. I would like you to accompany me to the races at Hialeah this afternoon." Having done his homework, finding that Vinni Peche was a regular at the tracks, Junie is sure of his answer.

"The offer is tempting."

"It's the least I can do after what I put you through."

"Well, okay, that sounds good; what about my friend?"

"Why don't we have a gentlemen's day out. She looks pretty content at the beach. Women bring me bad luck."

At the track, Junie drops hints about two people responsible for imprisoning and executing his relatives. Carl is not eager to respond, but anxious to learn more. "When were your relatives taken into custody?"

"Come to think of it, you may remember since it was in Chicago ten years ago. They were executed two years back."

"I do remember there were two informants and understand they have disappeared." Junie's ears perk up.

"Carl, my cousin in Sicily is on a vendetta to get these two. He has offered to pay a considerable amount of money to anyone leading him to their location. Do you happen to remember any names?" Now Vinni is intrigued. The magic phrase is "considerable amount of money."

"I remember two names: Chiabrera and Minotti."

"Those are the two. What if the two of us team up and try to find them for my cousin? I know he will be quite generous." The more the two talk, the more confidence Vinni has in his newly acquired friend. Could it be they are on the same mission? He is too wrapped up in the illusion of finding the two that he fails to see that the chance meeting with Junie Poeta was premeditated. They arrange to meet later in the evening to discuss if a plan should be considered to pursue a hunt.

Junie reflects on thoughts of his own to isolate Vinni from his female companion. He talks to his cousin Danny. "She may become a hazard. I don't know what he has told her or will confide. The fellow is cocky and likes to brag."

"How close do they appear?"

"He indicated they met just a few days ago."

"If she gets in the way, you know what to do. Just make it clean. Find out all you can that he knows."

The two criminal conspirators meet after dinner and exchange trusts. "Carl, I get a feeling that Carl Mori is not your name."

"It is while I am here."

"You look familiar. Were you recently in the paper?" Vinni, getting a little flustered, stays silent. "You don't have to worry about me. All I want is for us to work together and pool our assets of knowledge. I can tell you what I know about Minotti and Chiabrera and my thoughts of where they may be hiding, and you can do the same if you want a piece of the pie."

"Okay, I'm in."

"Good! Now how much have you told this Jane about yourself?"

"She thinks I am an undercover cop doing my duty."

"In order for us to work together, I think it best for you to end your relationship with her for the time being." Giving in to a feeling of intimidation by this charismatic and somewhat forceful suggestion, he agrees to do so. "Tell her your business is escalating to another level and it is not safe for a woman."

The meeting with Jane doesn't go well. He gives her money to take care of the car and more to compensate her for a few weeks. She, however, has become a little greedy and wishes to hang on to him, even though he tries convincing her he will call when his mission is accomplished. It becomes obvious to Junie that after she relocates to another hotel, she is spying on the two of them and not eager to leave the area. She is becoming suspicious.

Vinni has admitted his true identity to Poeta, who pretends not to have known and the two begin to share knowledge about the informants in hiding. Vinni is convinced that records exist that had belonged to two deceased doctors in Middleton, Georgia. "If we can get to those records, we will have a description of the faces we have to look for and possibly more. The plastic surgeon has a son with the FBI. I understand the son has made a career of tracking the people responsible for his father's death. He is close to a woman who is the daughter of Dr. Aldrich, the follow-up physician who died in an accident."

"Is this all the information you have? Where do you think those files are stored?"

"My theory is to force David Barr or Jennifer Aldrich to find them for us."

"How do you plan to do this?"

"Dr. Barr gave up his life rather than the files. Dr. Aldrich was also a martyr."

Vinni, a little stunned by the knowledge his new friend has of the demise of the two doctors who attended the informants hidden in seclusion, is reluctant to comment. He now realizes the state of devotion the Sicilian family has to eradicate Minotti and Chiabrera. The knowledge of this makes him aware that his so-called chance meeting with Poeta had been planned. "This is not the time to be reckless." These people are loyal only to one another within the family and will devitalize anyone standing in the way.

CHAPTER SEVENTY

Vinni wastes no time in telling Junie Poeta the background of his father and grandfather and their ties to Sicily, indicating that he probably has relatives living in the area. He has a compelling urgency to relate his ancestry. "We may be cousins," he says to Poeta, who expresses little enthusiasm.

"Vinni, let's put our heads together and chart a plan to get to the files. We know there are records in Georgia. The FBI stores records electronically. I believe some files to be in the hands of the relatives of the two doctors. They may not even know they have access to them."

"How do you think this?"

"Some time ago, during a relationship with one of the employees of the rehabilitation clinic in Middleton, I found out that the facial identities of two men who are now living out of the country, possibly in Central America, were changed."

International crime syndicates have started working together. The American Mafia or La Cosa Nostra and Sicilian Mafia have always worked separately, but are thought to have joined forces. This, according to Danny Moreno, is an asset in helping to find the two men if they are in South America. "It is too risky to take Peche's plan. Can he be of any use?"

"Not unless he gets a job with Interpol."

"Okay, wrap things up and get back here."

Two days later, Junie boarded a plane disguised as a priest. The *Miami Herald* printed a story about an unidentified woman found on the beach, a possible drowning victim. She was later identified as Jane Belmont, from Ohio, by a hotel employee. Junie never got around to liking Vinni Peche. He was discovered by a hysterical maid, with his hands and feet tied together, his throat cut, lying in a motel bathtub. Upon returning to Sicily, Cousin Danny asks, "Did you give him last rights?"

CHAPTER SEVENTY-ONE

Jennifer had just finished reading her mother's notes when David called. "Jen, I need to keep the records your mother left. They are of great importance. I promise to keep them in a safe place. I will explain when I see you."

"David, I have found out a lot more about my mother from her notes. When can we get together?"

"I have to take a trip with Hays to Florida. I'll be in touch in a couple of days. Try and have some fun while I'm gone. Call Marsha and help with her wedding plans."

"That is a great idea."

"Stay safe; I will see you soon."

Over a leisurely lunch the next day with Marsha, Jennifer shares her mother's life from the dossier she had left. "I have found that she sponsored two children in Guatemala. The notes she left tell me that a two-year-old girl and six-year-old boy she had met while on a medical journey had gotten close to her. The father's whereabouts were unknown and the mother was having a difficult time. I want to locate these children. I know she would want that."

"Jen, I think that is a wonderful thing to do."

"Also, I have her medical records and those of my grandparents, her parents. Her parents died when she was in her teens. She was sent to an orphanage and adopted by a medical doctor and her lawyer husband. This is where her inspiration to become a medical doctor originated. The couple was killed in an air disaster soon after she graduated from medical school. They left everything to her, but from her notes, I know she was devastated by losing them. She stated that in one breath she would give it all back, just to have them in her life for a little while longer. There were no goodbyes.

"In one of her journals, she expressed the fact that she had a few suitors, but concentrated on her work and was interested in poverty-stricken nations, especially the children that were affected. She wrote that the lack of mere subsistence such as food and shelter for the children of the world is appalling. She seemed to be so stricken by the thought of homeless and hungry people and told how she spends time at shelters feeding the homeless when she can on holidays. I remember doing that with her a few times."

"She sounds like a remarkable, caring woman. That must be where your spirit of giving and compassion come from."

CHAPTER SEVENTY-TWO

"Now, Marsha, let's talk about your wedding. I am so looking forward to seeing you in that gorgeous gown."

"Just a few more days and I will have a ready-made family. I hope I can be a good wife and a good mom to Art's two boys. They are such bright young men and so polite. He is a wonderful role model for them."

"You will do fine."

"What about you, Jen? I hoped you and David would be together. You appear to be so close to one another."

"Whatever happens, I will always love David. I spent just a few days with Rab and began to feel so comfortable with him, I didn't realize how attached I was beginning to become until he isn't around."

"What happened?"

"I saw his picture in the paper with a nurse from the hospital where he is chief surgeon. She was looking up at him like a hungry pelican. The two are obviously a couple. I decided to lick my wounds and go on. I do think of him occasionally. I sent him a letter, thanking him for the wonderful long weekend. He is such a gentleman. He called a few times, but I didn't want to complicate my life by answering."

"Jennifer, I cannot believe you. It isn't wise to assume he is in a relationship. You could be wrong."

"Well, it is over the dam by now." Realizing Jennifer has gotten a little tense over the subject, Marsha suggests they go to the health spa to work out and have a massage. The rest of the afternoon is devoted to wedding arrangements made for Marsha and Art, their plan for a honeymoon and where they will be living.

David and Agent Hayes returned from Florida after spending time at the morgue and with the local police. Forensics will determine if the body of the man found in the motel bathtub is a wanted felon. The drowning victim, whose picture was in the paper, was identified as having been seen with him by the same maid who discovered the body of Carl Mori. The night clerk told of another gentleman seen with the couple and again alone with Mr. Mori. He was able to give a good description. However, with the many disguises used by Junie Poeta, he will be hard to locate, especially in another country.

It is a rainy fall day when David contacts Jennifer at the hospital. "Jen, I just returned and thought we might get together. If you have a little time, I could run by the hospital for a brief lunch."

"I'm sorry, David. I can't take any time until later. Can you come by this evening?"

"Sure, that might work out better anyway. What if I bring dinner?"

"Why don't I make dinner and you bring the wine."

"Great! See you at 7:00."

During dinner, they discussed the notes that Jennifer's mother had left and experiences of her life detailed in the journals. "Jen, the documents that your mother left are the ones she told you in her letter are secret. They are the initial records of both doctors, sworn to secrecy about the two men in the witness program. The photographs show the before and after pictures of the facial changes and must be kept in a place or destroyed. I have seen these two men and know the pictures to be legitimate. We can take no chances for these photos to be stolen.

I believe you were abducted to force knowledge of the documents and having them in your possession would put you in grave danger. This is probably what got both our parents killed."

"I understand. What dangers do we have to look for now?"

"We believe that Peche has been murdered. That is why I went to Florida. We are waiting for the forensics lab to complete some tests. By the way, I called Rab while I was in Lauderdale. He asked about you."

"You did? How he is?"

"He seems to be fine. We were going to get together, but his schedule wouldn't permit it this time. He thinks we are a couple."

"Oh? Well, I guess it doesn't matter one way or another."

"It does to me, Jen, and I'm pretty sure it does to him."

"What do you mean?"

"I think the two of you had a misunderstanding about the status of relationships. You should give him a call." Jen makes no comment. "By the way, I believe your birthday is coming up soon and I want to know if you would do me the honor of going out with me on a dinner date."

"Thank you, David, I would love that."

"Good! I will make the arrangements. Until then, I have to be out of town for a few days and will get with you when I get back."

"I imagine, like always, you can't say where you are going." He smiles and kisses her on the forehead before leaving. "David, please be careful."

Chapter Seventy-Three

David's second trip to Belize took him back to the airport in Lady-ville, ten miles from Belize City, where he was again acquainted with the cab driver whom he had met previously. The two exchanged pleasantries before driving to Cayo, the largest of six districts. The districts are Corozal, Orange Walk, Belize, Cayo, Stann Creek, and Toledo. The drive is about an hour away. Max, the driver, knows something about all the districts and is eager to share his knowledge about the area's ancient coral beds, limestone formations, and all the natural wonders that made David's trip informative and pleasurable.

The overall climate is sub-tropical, with high humidity disguised by cooling sea breezes. On this day, the wind is light, the temperature is bordering seventy degrees, and the rainfall is light.

In September, the northern part of the country receives five to seven inches of rain, whereas the rain is considerably heavier in the district of Toledo, lasting three days at a time. Most of the rain falls on the mountains.

The wind in the area of the Gulf of Mexico and southwestern plains is called the northers, bringing in cold air from the north, which meets warmer tropical air over Belize in October, causing rainfall and heavy winds.

Special Operations, including the Central Intelligence Agency, foreign government, and Interpol, working to inform the FBI, uncovered information that Sicilian mobsters noted for violent kidnappings are on the trail of Chiabrera and Minotti. Their aliases of Vincent Carlos and Aldo Tripoli are vulnerable and they are in jeopardy of being discovered by a group headed by Danny Morino, a *solon* of the Sicilian Mafioso in Palermo. The CIA uncovered information that the group is on a vendetta for revenge and planning to go to Central America on what they call a religious mission.

David explains to Max that he is on vacation this trip although his intelligence tells him that Max has the mental ability to perceive differently. They smile sheepishly at one another and Max departs.

David rents a cabin in a remote fishing village to await the arrival of Jake Jaffey, the former counterintelligence agent he had worked with before. The plan is to rent a fifteen-passenger van and pick up a special units task force flying in from the states by a special plane. They will be ready when Danny Moreno and his missionaries arrive.

David's unexpected meeting with Vincent Carlos and Aldo Tripoli was brief and to the point. "The two of you are in danger and must leave the area immediately. I am here to take you to a safer place. There won't be much time to prepare; tell your business associates you will be out of town for a few days, pack a few clothes, and be prepared to leave as soon as possible. Tomorrow may be too late." The two men, as calmly as they could, tell their employees they have been called on some unexpected business and will return in a couple of days; until then, the office will be closed. David, Jake, and the two men leave an hour later in a van presumed on route to the airport. The winds have picked up and the rainfall is more determined on the trip to Cayo.

CHAPTER SEVENTY-FOUR

David explains to the two men, who by this time are more than anxious to know what is happening, that a group from Palermo is seeking revenge and may have an idea of their location. "The two of you will be confined to a cabin in an area where we will be operating a command post. We will do everything possible to protect you, as well as ourselves." The two men, aware that these agents are risking their own safety, will cooperate to the fullest.

In the early hours Sunday morning when all is dark and quiet, a plane flies over a sparsely populated area in Belize. The Belizean farmers are not out harvesting corn or planting beans as they do during the week this time of year. More than half of the people live in rural areas and are of multiracial descent.

Ten parachutes float toward the damp ground. The rain is slight and the winds are not strong enough to interfere with target landing. The ten special forces gather and fold their chutes before they quickly approach the large van where David and Jake are waiting. Back at the command post, they are briefed as to what is expected to happen. David lays out a plan of interference when the Sicilian Mafioso arrives as expected within the next twenty-four hours. The information comes from a counterintelligence agent who has managed to take an aggressive approach, learning from informants and wiretaps about important targets.

Six members of Danny Moreno's organization, including Danny himself and two of his cousins, are in route to the coastal area of Belize. The informant advised that the mob is interested in looking at an import-export business in the city of Belize believed to be operated by two partners not from the area. They do not have solid proof that the two businessmen are Minotti and Chiabrera, but it won't take long for them to figure it out once they arrive at the city of Belize. They have done their homework and are visibly dedicated to martyrdom. A Mafia recruit is sworn to secrecy, and vows, in Italian, "I enter this organization to protect my family and to protect all my friends. I swear not to divulge this secret and to obey, with love and *omerta*." *Omerta* refers to the Mafia's code of silence. "We get in alive and the only way out is dead." They also vow not to cooperate with law enforcement.

It is close to midnight Sunday; the first week of October, strong northers blow across the Maya Mountains. An urgent call comes in to Agent David Barr. "Four men have just embarked from Philip S. Golden International Airport. They are in route to Belize City by bus. We will keep you posted." David immediately informs his team, including the agents at the import-export business operated by the men in hiding. The four men check in at a luxury hotel in Belize City, have dinner, and are not visible the rest of the night.

Chapter Seventy-Five

Monday morning, two of the men staying at the hotel are observed renting motorcycles. The remaining two are watched as they enjoy a leisurely breakfast in the hotel dining area. An hour later, all four get together in one of the suite rooms for two hours before surfacing. Thus far, they have made no illegal moves and will be watched closely.

While David waits in the gray, damp air on an increasingly chilly day for any change of venue, he receives a phone call from the states. "Agent Barr, we have confirmation from the FBI lab that Vinni Peche is the victim found in the bathtub in Florida."

"Good work. Thanks." This knowledge confirms what the FBI thought from the time Peche was discovered. The group from Palermo found out all they could from Peche and wasted him.

David and his team, with the support of local government officials who have been informed of expected drug deals, are on lookout. Airstrips are being watched, as well as waterways and rental agencies. Anything suspicious will be reported to Agent Barr or a member of his team. Two agents posing as business executives are placed at the offices of Carlos and Tripoli. Two more are used as back-up. The receptionist often works when the office is closed. She has been given a paid vacation.

Early afternoon, a fishing boat leaves San Pedro, located on the southern tip of Ambergris Caye. San Pedro is the hub of activity on Ambergris Caye and forty miles northeast of Belize City. San Pedro's inhabitants are mostly of Mexican descent and speak both English and Spanish. They are said to be knowledgeable and responsible people. A couple of diving guides became aware of the suspicious fishing boat and notified local authorities. Four men seen on board were dressed as fishermen, except for the shoes one was wearing that appeared to be from an expensive designer. Equipment concealed in boxes were claimed to be fishing gear and clothing. The observant guides, who are constantly on water and in touch with local fishermen as well as tourists, became concerned that this is out of the ordinary.

When the news reached Belize, David deployed men at the corners of the streets in view of the business under surveillance. Some were positioned up on the rooftops.

The grave reality of the Sicilian Mafia is the violent killings. They oppose authority and in the earlier days murdered thousands of men of honor, including business executives and media and political figures. They controlled and influenced the economy.

Governments responded with a mutual action of opposing force and countertendency, exhausting the power of the murderous alliance. Emerging again in 2004, the Sicilian Mafia once again gained momentum in horrific acts of violence.

CHAPTER SEVENTY-SIX

The rain is light and the evening is quietly filled with the hum of anticipation among the small army of protectors. The small fishing vessel was docked at a secluded reef of sand on the edge of Belize City. Four men emerged and waited aboard the craft as a van accelerated into traffic in route to their location. Fortunately, they are unaware of a small car not far behind with two Interpol agents watching their every move. When the van came into view, the four men aboard the boat prepared to depart, wearing what appeared to be combat clothing. They make no attempt to hide weapons. David and the FBI agents are notified and lie in wait. It is necessary to gather intelligence on activities of any criminal before moving in. The key is to not wait too long before acting. David joins the four agents inside the warehouse offices of Tripoli and Carlos. The men posted on both sides of the street moved forward after the van stopped at the back entrance of the building. Six men dressed for destruction were prepared to identify and destroy Giacomo Minotti and Luigi Chiabrera, the traitors to their family. They had been tipped off by generously tipping a hotel porter that the two men operating the business often worked late. Therefore, they expected the lights to be shining in the building, directing them to their targets. Just as the rear office door caved in, one of David's well-placed agents swiveled around in an office chair, blowing a hole through the chest of one of Danny's men in self defense. The man was positioned to trigger a machine gun. The group from Palermo, white with terror, fired shots at shadows. They knew they had been set up and at the same time realized they had uncovered the identities of the two hunted men. The fugitives spread out in an effort to fight and complete their mission, but are ill prepared for the precision at which the FBI is trained to protect. David surprised a man in the hall that he recognized as the person he suspected to have run his motorcycle off the road in Georgia. He, along with three others, was promptly handed over to the local authorities, who had surrounded the building in a National-Guard-like defense. Danny Moreno was identified as the head of the organization, but had slipped out of sight, as did his cousin, Junie Poeta. The evening became night and the two are on the loose. The building is large with many storage areas and empty containers for shipping. There is only a remote possibility that they could have escaped in the confusion of gunfire.

David is determined more than ever that he has an opportunity to, at last, bring his father's killer to a triumphant capture. He is exhilarated at the thought, while he continues to search the building with Jake and the rest of the team. Inch by inch, they search, hoping beyond all hope that the two have not gotten away, when a small sound of a muffled cough is heard from a large barrel. They motion to one another. "Which one?" They stand quietly staring at twelve barrels as the pounding rain stampedes the rooftop. Finally, Junie Poeta is unable to camouflage his allergy to the grain inside the confinement of the barrel. He throws open the lid, gasping for breath, and aimlessly fires at the surrounding forces. David is hit in the jugal or upper cheek. He is immediately taken out of harm's way while Junie Poeta ends his life of crime, buried in a bloody barrel of grain. Jake and the others extend the search, vigorously knocking all the barrels to the concrete floor. Danny Moreno, realizing he is out-numbered and losing his grip from overhead rafters, emerges from his hiding place begging for his life, as he crawls toward Jake and the others, who are pointing every available ammunition at his head. David, dazed and bleeding from the face, stands up and stares at the man who took his father's life and most likely the life of Jennifer's mother. Without saying a word, he feels the most gratifying achievement of his entire career. David was whisked away to the local hospital. The extent of his injury is, although not life-threatening, in need of immediate attention. Jake is put in charge to make all the arrangements to expedite the bodies back to Palermo. The others are in federal custody and will face international criminal charges, including drug trafficking, murder, attempted murder and a host of other charges that will be proven in a court of law.

Chapter Seventy-Seven

Vincent Carlos and Aldo Tripoli have two choices. They can be relocated with new names or stay where they are, considering the fact that the most danger to them is over with the head of a threatening Mafia family in custody facing a death penalty. Also, the fact that Vinni Peche is no longer a threat will give them minimum reason to fear. It is a helpful thing when the bad guys eliminate one another.

Jake escorted David back to the states. The bullet fragment is painfully present in his face, but surgery can wait until he returns home. As they rode in Max's cab to the airport, Max gave them a copy of the local paper, which told about a gang of drug dealers and most wanted Mafia figures who were intercepted by the FBI breaking into a local business. Max, looking at David's bandaged face, asks if he is okay and thanks him for coming, as if he knows he was there to clean up corruption.

Upon arrival in the states, David makes a quick call to his mother and then to Jen. "I have finished my business without much incident, just a scratch on my face, and am on my way home." He has always been in the habit of minimizing threats on his life to his mother.

The newspapers in the states tell much more of the story. International crime affecting Americans is a focus of the FBI. These particular crime figures have been under a close vigil by the legal attaché for a number of years. Suspecting the crime figures of committing heinous crimes in the United States, they now have proof. The media told of one FBI agent severely injured, but did not give his name.

In the society section of the paper on the same day of the breaking story in Belize was the notice of Marsha Benning and Art Cantrell's wedding plans. "That is right around the corner, Jen," David comments to Jennifer.

"Yes, but my concern is the bullet hole in your face." The two have an unbreakable bond and truly love each other. "I am taking you to the best plastic surgeon, other than Dr. Barr, of course, that I know of." David, trusting her expertise in the field she knows, asks her to make the arrangements.

"You are a very lucky man, Mr. Barr. This bullet came close to putting your eye out."

The surgery, performed by Dr. Garnet, went well. "Part of the bone is damaged and had to be reconstructed as well. You should have very little scarring. It should heal nicely within a few weeks. It penetrated quite deep into the bone, and…as I have said, you are one lucky man. That bullet went through something else with great force before it got to you."

CHAPTER SEVENTY-EIGHT

David took a couple of weeks to recuperate at the insistence of the bureau. This gives him time to plan a small birthday party for Jen and to attend the upcoming wedding as best man along with Art's two teenage sons, ages thirteen and fifteen, who will be groomsmen.

The next week, David is feeling better; the pain in his wound is much easier now without the pain killers. The fall days in Middleton are warm and beautiful, with plenty of sunshine. David and his mother plan a small dinner party to include Marsha, Art, and a couple of Jennifer's favorite friends, Ms. Klara and Dr. Kleinman, to celebrate Jen's birthday. The dinner conversation is diverted from David's recent experience to honeymoon plans. Marsha and Art plan to go back to the beach house belonging to David's friend. Simon Cohen insisted on giving them this for a wedding gift. After all, that is where it all began. Birthday cake was served and a few special gifts were given to Jen, including a diamond pendant from David, before the evening came to an early end and Jen was escorted home by Dr. Kleinman and Ms. Klara.

The next couple of days were the usual customary bridal shower, last-minute wedding details, and a rehearsal dinner. There was no mention of a bachelor party. Art had lived through that once. However, this is Marsha's first and hopefully only marriage. She is overwhelmed with excitement. With all the threats behind, she and Jennifer have time to relax and talk about the future.

CHAPTER SEVENTY-NINE

The day of the wedding has finally arrived. It is a beautiful Saturday with no rain in sight, as a cool morning breeze purifies the calming air warmed by rays of the sun. Marsha is a beautiful woman and is radiant in her wedding gown. Jennifer is stunning as well. David, as always the handsome prince-like figure in Jen's life, is getting admiring glances from several ladies, even with the rather obvious bandage on his cheek. He and Art look like distinguished male models in the tuxedos they are wearing. Two pretty young nieces, children of Marsha's brother paired with Art's handsome young boys, complete the wedding party.

The ceremony ends and David escorts Jen behind the newly married couple down the white carpet toward the entrance of the church. As Jen looks toward the back of the church on the side of the groom, it was like all the air had left the room. She had gotten a glimpse of Dr. Rab Bharne, a sober admiring smile on his face. "David, Dr. Bharne is here."

"Yes, I know; I invited him."

"Why? He doesn't know Marsha or Art, does he?"

"He is my friend and my date."

"David, don't be funny."

"Okay, he and I have become acquainted and have some business to take care of." Puzzled, Jen joins the reception line and waits for a more opportune time to have more questions.

When Rab approaches, he is introduced to the bridal couple as a friend of the family by David. "Hello, Jennifer. It is so good to see you; you look wonderful." He gently kisses the back of her hand and disappears into the crowd.

"Jen, close your mouth!"

"David, you are starting to scare me." She gently kicks him.

The reception gets underway and a small group of musicians are playing big band music. There is no rock and roll, at least not yet. The younger adults may have some requests. After everyone arrives, David makes a beautiful speech about the groom and the relationship he himself has shared with the new bride, working together.

The bride and groom share the first dance, after which David escorts Jen onto the dance floor. Rab cannot help to see what a beautiful couple they make. He joins in a casual conversation with some of the guests, when David brings Jen over to him. "Rab, it is so good of you to come. Would you do me the honor...of dancing with my sister?"

ABOUT THE AUTHOR

A native of Middletown Ohio, the author, Barbara Nelson, now resides with her family in Louisville, KY. She has been published in various newspaper and magazine articles. After a career in business management and related fields, Barbara is now focused full time on her first love, the written word. She is presently in the process of completing yet another novel and developing ongoing literary projects.

Printed in the United States
77662LV00003B/244-252

9 781434 308399